Fool's Paradise

SALLY SUMMERS

Heartline
Books

Published by Heartline Books Limited in 2002

Copyright © Sally Summers 2002

Sally Summers has asserted her rights under the Copyright, Designs and Patents Act, 1988 to be identified as the author of this work.

First published in the United Kingdom in 2002 by Heartline Books Limited.

Heartline Books Limited
PO Box 22598, London W8 7GB

Heartline Books Ltd. Reg No: 03986653

ISBN 1-903867-43-6

Styled by Oxford Designers & Illustrators

Printed and bound in Great Britain by
Cox & Wyman, Reading, Berkshire

SALLY SUMMERS

SALLY SUMMERS is a freelance writer of short stories, essays, and articles, and has been widely published in Australia, the U.K., and the U.S.A. She also worked as an advertising copywriter, but gave it up after 'research' when working on a campaign for a chocolate company caused her to gain three and a half kilos.

Her very first story, written when she was six years old, was a romance: it was about two pumpkin seeds who fall in love. Later, she was inspired by her romance-addicted grandmother's passion for the books she read endlessly. Sally thought it would be a great gift to be able to transport readers like her grandmother on an emotional journey they would enjoy and remember. Her first attempt had the makings for a forgettable trip rather than a memorable journey, so she put her efforts aside for a few years, until she could tackle them with a fresh perspective. *Fool's Paradise* is her first romantic novel, and she credits her love of the characters for making the writing of it such a pleasure.

Sally lives in Australia, and divides her time between her lakeside home in country Victoria, and her weekend getaway in Melbourne. Some people get away from the city on the weekends, but Sally prefers to go against the flow, even if the flow is only traffic. Her favourite pastime – other than being with her husband and family – is to ride her Vespa with earphones on under her helmet, music blasting, and sea wind on her face.

Heartline Books –
Romance at its best

Call the Heartline Hotline on 0845 6000 504 and order any book you may have missed – you can now pay over the phone by credit or debit card.

Have you visited the Heartline website yet?

If you haven't – and even for those of you who have – it's well worth a trip as we are constantly updating our site.

So log on to <u>www.heartlinebooks.com</u> where you can…

- ♥ Order one or more books – including titles you may have missed – and pay by credit or debit card
- ♥ Check out special offers and events, such as celebrity interviews
- ♥ Find details of our writing classes for aspiring authors
- ♥ Read more about Heartline authors
- ♥ Enter competitions
- ♥ Browse through our catalogue

And much, much more…

prologue

Friday 13 November 1987

In her long velvet gown, wearing fake pearls and a rhinestone tiara on the mass of red curls on her head, Cara St John made for a very convincing Elizabeth I. Convincing, that is, except for the fact that her shoulders couldn't help moving to the beat coming from inside the Toongalla High School Hall, as Billy Idol rebel-yelled 'More, more, more!'

Inside, at the Year Twelve costume ball, students celebrated not just the end of the year but the end of an era. Next week, exams would begin, and destinies would be forged. For Cara, her destiny involved getting the hell out of Toongalla. She was going to be a newspaper journalist. A really good one. And one day, she would be the *best* one.

Her destiny also involved the gorgeous and desirable Evan Worthington, which was why she was out here in the warm night air, listening to the cicadas giving Billy Idol a run for his money, and walking among couples who leaned into each other, whispering lovers' secrets, some of them entwined in passionate clinches that not even the bravest of the ambulating chaperones were game to untangle. She smiled to herself. Pretty soon she'd be one of them too. And to think that she had Daniel Hunter to thank for this! And all Dan had to do, for her life to snap into focus, was to leave Toongalla for the 'Big Smoke' at the start of the year.

Big Smoke, or up in smoke, she didn't care! Without

Dan Hunter forever making jokes and snide remarks at her expense, suddenly she wasn't quiet, geeky 'Carrot-top' any more, but simply Cara, and she had blossomed, free to pursue her interests and goals and… Evan!

Tonight was the night. Already Cara and Evan – a dashing Count Dracula, with a sexy black satin mask over his face – had spent an hour on the dance floor, hips locked, looking into each other's eyes, swaying languorously through each song fast and slow. When she had pleaded for a break and gone to the loo, Evan had sent a message that he would meet her outside. Oh yes, this was it all right.

Cautiously, Cara began to walk down the path that led down the side of the school, her heartbeat becoming louder in her ears as the music from the hall became fainter. Suddenly someone took her arm, and pulled her into the tea-tree bushes against the fence. She had no time to scream out her surprise, for once in there, her captor enveloped her in his cape and brought persuasive lips to her own.

The only coherent thought she had before surrendering to the assault on her senses, was that this was her first, grown-up kiss. There was no fumbling, no groping, just a man and a woman perfectly attuned to the music of their hearts, as their mouths moved together in a long, slow, achingly sensual dance that was earning a standing ovation from each and every one of her hormones.

A soft moan escaped her as the kiss shifted up a gear and her pulse rate went with it, sending a gush of raw need through her. Her hands, seemingly of their own volition, shifted from his chest to his back, and down, down, until they were on deliciously muscular buttocks that she cupped and squeezed hard. Under her touch, he too moaned, and moved his hands down the length of her until they were on the back of her thighs. With a show of strength that made her gasp against his lips, he effortlessly lifted her on to the fence. Every inhibition, which had made her the quiet studious type all these years, was cast off as she wound long slender legs around his waist and pulled him to her, smiling in womanly confidence as he broke the kiss and took her face in his hands, panting slightly. He was delicious, and she was going to devour him.

'I knew that with that red hair, you must be a wild one, Carrot-top.'

Cara shook her head, as if to clear it. What was wrong with this picture? She knew that voice, and she knew that detestable nickname, but they didn't fit this situation. Some quick calculations were in order. There was only one person who had that voice, and only one person who called her 'Carrot-top', and only one person who was as tall as Evan Worthington, so that meant she now had her legs wrapped around...

'Dan!'

He stroked her still pleasurably tingling lips with a gentle thumb. 'It's OK, baby. I just thought we'd better slow it down a bit...'

'But...but...you're Dan!'

'Of course. Who did you think I was?'

Cara clenched her fists and teeth. He had led her on! Well, no, actually he hadn't, he had never said he was Evan, but...jeez! She had nearly devoured Dan Hunter! Dan Hunter – yuk!

'I...I really have to go now.'

She hopped down from the fence and tried pushing past him, but he grabbed her arm. Cara's brain hadn't quite let her body in on this new information, and she felt a mortifying fresh surge of desire under his touch. Determined to leave, she tipped a mental bucket of ice water over herself and tugged her arm away.

'Carrot-top, you didn't think I was someone else, did you?'

His grin, as always, was gorgeous, but wicked, totally wicked. The Dracula costume suited him right down to the ground. 'Someone like…Evan Worthington perhaps?'

Cara's mouth and eyes opened in disbelief as realisation hit her.

'You did this on purpose!'

Dan saw her realisation turn to fury, and put up his palms in placation, delivering an explanation at a speed that would have impressed a livestock auctioneer.

'Now, Carrot-top, you know I never said that I was Evan. It's not my fault that just because I happened to be in Toongalla this weekend and was given a ticket to the ball, you assumed that because I'm tall I must be him…'

Cara put her hands on his chest, and gave a mighty shove. He sprawled into the tea-tree bushes, arms and legs akimbo. Once he was down, she stabbed his chest with an index finger that punctuated her every word.

'Low-down. Dirty. Scumbag. You. Knew. Exactly. What. You. Were. Doing!'

'Ow! No, I…Ow! I hoped to get you to myself, but you know why!'

'Yeah, I know why – because you are a childish psychopath whose entire reason for living is to find new ways to torment me!'

Dan sighed and his sudden, pained look made Cara's heart inexplicably contract.

'Cara, you know it wasn't always like that.' His voice was gentle, and it cut her deeper that any of his loud jibes ever had, because she *did* know, she *did* remember. 'I've been gone all year and I miss you so much…'

A little something within her broke away and soared

free for an instant before Cara threw a net over it and dragged it back down to earth. Dan, miss her? No way. It was more likely that he missed the power play. It couldn't be easy to find someone else willing to put up with his particular brand of nonsense.

'I must be about to die from the shock, because my life is flashing before me. And funnily enough, each and every one of those flashes features you making my life hell!'

'Just give me a chance, that's all I ask.'

'A chance? You know what they say, Dan – never let a fool kiss you, and never let a kiss fool you. I've done one of those tonight, and there's no way I'm going to be doing the other.'

Holding on to the tattered shreds of her remaining dignity, she lifted her chin, turned, and strode away.

'Wait! Hey, Cara, stop!' There was a loud rustling behind her from the squashed tea-tree as Dan stood up, but she kept walking.

'Really, you have to stop. I'm serious!' He called again, and she heard his footfall quicken as he began to run.

'Serious? That's a first! Just go away, will you Dan? There's a good boy.'

There was a loud stomp and Cara slammed to a halt, restrained by a force that made a choke chain seem gentle. After a puzzling split second, she quickly glanced back and realised that it was Dan, stepping on the train of her dress. But it would take more than that for her to stick around – something like wild elephants! She gritted her teeth and pulled with all her might, mentally wincing as she heard the lovely velvet rip behind her. She picked up her skirts, and ran. *Eat my dust, Hunter.*

'Stop! Cara, you don't understand! Y-you…'

Suddenly Dan stopped calling, and in its place was

something that chilled her to the very bone on this balmy night. Laughter. Mocking laughter, floating in the air all around her and then reverberating in her head, reproaching her for wanting to believe, even for a split second, that he had missed her. That he thought she was worth anything other than his ridicule and contempt. That she would have given him the pearl of her womanhood…when he was nothing but a swine. She took a deep breath and was shocked when it collided with a sob erupting from her throat. But she quashed the pain, quashed it small, and swept back inside, determined to have a good time.

She plastered a smile on her face and made her way to the dance floor, joining the throng in doing 'The Timewarp' again and again. It wasn't until her closest friends saw her and dragged her back into the loo, that she discovered Dan's crowning achievement. She had left the entire back of her skirt under Dan's shoe in the yard outside, and for the past ten minutes had been showing her behind to all the Year Twelve students, their parents, and their teachers!

chapter one

'No, I will *not* do it.' Cara's tone was polite but firm.

Brian 'Hutch' Hutchence took his glasses off and stared at her. That infamous look was enough to send any lesser newspaper staff-member scuttling, but Cara stared back. She had her own version of The Look.

'You may well be one of our finest journalists, but don't forget who you're speaking to!' Hutch said.

'OK. I won't do it, Sir!'

Hutch threw his arms up in the air, got up off his swivel chair, and started pacing. And ranting. He knew his voice could be heard through the glass door, and on through the entire floor.

'This is an exclusive for the *Clarion*! Daniel Hunter is Australia's favourite son! And Dan's returning home – triumphant!'

Cara crossed her arms and expelled an exasperated sigh. 'Yeah, well, then Australia's suffering from collective sunstroke. The man goes away for seven years, makes a few hit movies in Hollywood, and all of a sudden everyone wants to adopt him.'

'Not true! He's paid his dues doing the stand-up circuits, *and* he's talented.'

'If he's talented, then I'm Hemingway.'

'Really?' Hutch stood in front of Cara, hands on hips. 'Then tell me, Papa, which of his movies have you seen?'

Cara tried to look as though she was giving it serious thought. 'I've seen the previews.'

'Oh, come on…'

'They're enough. Beats me why, all of a sudden, this man is the coolest thing since whale-watching in the Antarctic?'

Hutch pointed a finger at her. 'You know why. He's given manufacturing licenses for "Mikhail McHale" merchandise to Australian-owned companies exclusively. He's a hero! You've gotta love the guy.'

'Well, *I* don't.'

Damn, she is stubborn, Hutch thought. They'd been offered an exclusive. A journalist could tag along for an entire week during Dan Hunter's promotional tour – and Cara was the only person for the job. Literally.

'Oh, come on, Cara.' He tried smiling, thinking that if she wouldn't be bullied, then maybe she could be cajoled. Hell, he was even prepared to bribe her. 'You know you're my best journalist.'

Cara ran a hand through her smooth red hair. 'Well, even if I was…'

'Which you are.'

'Which I'm *not*,' she paused, looking askance at him, 'I'm a serious journalist, and I cover the serious issues.'

'Well, if you're so serious, why are you behaving like a kid? This is exactly what you were like back in Toongalla.'

Cara's eyes widened and she lifted up an index finger in warning.

'Don't mention Toongalla.'

'Why not? I know you don't like to let it be known that, before you came to Brisbane I was your Uncle Hutch, but that makes me the person who's known you the longest in this city, and I know exactly why you're refusing the assignment. Can't you let bygones be bygones?'

'I have no idea what you're talking about.'

Hutch crossed his arms and looked at her through narrowed eyes.

'Oh, you know exactly what I'm talking about.'

Cara glared at him, biting her lip, and then looked away. A victory, but just a small one. He never would have guessed that convincing Cara to cover Dan's tour would be so difficult, or that her hurt would run so deep. And make no mistake, this was hurt, much as she tried to hide it in this splintery armour of sarcasm, disdain, and professional indignation. Hutch was Cara's father's best friend, and he had known her from the time she was born. Indeed, he knew her all too well, and was privy to all kinds of information that she liked to keep secret.

Dan and Cara had grown up together. On Davey Street, in the coastal town of Toongalla, they had been neighbours from birth, their relationship nurtured by their parents' close friendship. Cara, the St John's only child, got counted in on everything the Hunter tribe did. On picnics, barbecues, football outings, and trips to the beach, Cara joined in with the nine Hunter kids, and Denise Hunter, when making a head count, always counted to ten. If by rare chance Cara wasn't there, she'd turn to her husband Wayne and ask, 'Who's missing?'

Everyone at the time agreed that the relationship between Cara and Dan was special. Dan was a year older than Cara, a difference small enough for them to share everything – his Tonka trucks, her tea set, and one drooly juice bottle – and large enough for him to be fiercely protective of her. And then love, as the saying goes, had ruined a perfectly beautiful relationship.

Dan's actions, as childishly stupid as they'd been, were those of a young man head over heels in love, too immature to know how to show it. And Cara's hurt, well…it wasn't indifference, was it? A person who didn't care about Dan, a person who had chosen to discount the past because it had no bearing on the present, would shrug and think about how such an exclusive would look on her CV. But not Cara.

This was just one of the secrets Hutch was privy to. Another pretty big one was the reason why it was so important that she take the assignment in the first place.

'All right,' he sighed, suddenly weary. A looming election, a notorious criminal released from jail, trouble brewing in the Middle East, and here he was, trying to get an actor and a journo together. 'Let's say you're my worst journalist. You're still the best person for the job.'

'No, I'm not. This is nowhere near my field. Why isn't Entertainment covering this?' Cara opened the door and stuck her head out into the newsroom. 'Hey, Joey!' she called out. 'You'll cover the Dan Hunter tour, won't you?'

Joey chuckled humourlessly. 'Give me a break. It's all I can do to keep up with his publicist. I tell you, she won't be happy until I write the articles in my own blood.'

'Look,' Hutch murmured discreetly, 'I know entertainment isn't your thing. This doesn't have to be given the entertainment angle…'

'Ah, of course. Art. Hey, Melina!' she called out to the Arts Supplement Editor. 'You'll cover Dan Hunter, won't you?'

'"Mikhail McHale, Double Agent" is to art what colonic irrigation is to entertainment!'

'See what I'm up against?' Hutch smiled at Cara.

'You've got a hard job ahead of you, Hutch,' she smiled back, straightening his crooked tie. 'Be gentle on them.'

'Wait!' Hutch called out to her retreating form. 'I'll pay you freelancer rates!'

Cara turned around and waved. 'Thanks, Hutch, but you know the *Clarion*'s wages are fit for a queen. See you Monday.'

'That's if there is a job waiting for you Monday…!'
'Byeeee!'

Cara snatched up her briefcase, handbag, and bottle of water, making sure she looked the perfect picture of cool and nonchalance. Once out of sight, however, she ran to the lift as fast as her heels and narrow skirt would allow, her heart racing and with palms so sweaty that she could barely keep a grip on her briefcase and water bottle.

Hutch and Cara's creative differences sometimes made for lively discussion, but their relationship was mutually respectful. Never, never in a million years would she normally have done what she'd just done to escape the Dan Hunter job. After all, she thought, I am the consummate professional. At least – I *was*.

She took a swig of water, miserably wishing it were something stronger. The only use she had for water right now was to dump it on her head.

Of course, she knew Dan was in town. She had known he was coming for months, courtesy of her mother.

'Honey,' her mother had said over the phone just last week, 'I was talking to Denise just today, and guess what? Dan is coming in just a few days!'

'Really?' Cara had said mildly, thankful that ordinary telephones didn't yet register rolling eyes, pulling faces, and stifling fake yawns. Some part of her was shocked at her behaviour whenever Dan's name was mentioned, but he did that to her, dammit! The mere thought of Dan always demoted her from a respected 32-year-old journalist to some silly teenager.

'Yes, really. Isn't it wonderful! Denise and Wayne will be having a big barbecue for him. Everyone will be there, and you know Dan would love to see you. Denise says he always asks after you. And, you know, we haven't seen you in a few months ourselves either. Come home, touch base, and catch up with us. You need some rest and relaxation, something normal and homely and not even vaguely connected to politics or wars or land rights or nuclear testing. Carrying the weight of the world on your shoulders, I think, no wonder you're looking so peaky. If you ask me, you could do with a bit of a laugh, a drink, and a good rare steak. Are you still not eating red meat? It's full of iron, you know. Please come – it'll do you a world of good…'

And so she had gone on and on, while Cara opened her mail, made herself a cup of coffee, and painted nail-polish on her fingernails *and* toenails, every now and then emitting a small non-committed noise like 'Mmm hmm?' and 'Oh?' so her mother would know that her brain hadn't imploded in the sudden vacuum of her mind. She didn't want the low-down on Dan from her mother, or anyone else. The only benefit in knowing what his movements were going to be was so that Cara could make sure she was exactly where *he wasn't*.

But despite being unable to escape all the hype or Mum's gossip about Dan, it had been easy all these years to avoid the dreaded man himself. And now Hutch wanted her to spend an entire week with him! She would not do it. It was a matter of principle. Unfortunately, she gulped painfully, that little principle had just cost her her job.

Oh boy, she thought, *this weekend is going to need some heavy artillery. I need videos. Enough for the entire weekend. And chocolate. Lots of it.*

Pounding. Hammering.

Cara opened her eyes to a cautious squint, trying to work out where the noise was coming from. She shook her head, trying to clear it. It was a bad move.

'Ow!' she yelped, as pain shot up her neck and shoulders, the instant karma of falling asleep on the sofa with her head on the armrest.

'Cara, we know you're there. Open up!'

It was Pia's voice. What time was it? She blinked at her watch. Eleven o'clock in the morning!

'Coming...' she croaked.

Ugh. She didn't feel well. At her feet lay empty food wrappers, and the television was turned to the midnight-to-noon music programme. It was the heavy metal hour. *Jeez, I must have been out of it to sleep through this*, Cara thought, putting a screaming guitar out of its misery with the 'off' button. The last thing she could remember was putting on the sixth video, and frying – then eating – rösti potatoes for one...which was clearly why she was now feeling so sick. There was a quarter of a pound of butter sitting in her stomach, showing no signs of wanting to be digested.

Cara caught a glimpse of herself in the hallway mirror before she opened the door. Ugh! If it wasn't her best friends who were knocking, she would have hidden under the bed with all the other scary monsters.

Pound, pound, pound. Cara opened the door, and caught Pia mid-knock.

'Well! About time!' Pia breezed past her into the living room.

Lucie put a hand on Cara's cheek, feeling her temperature. 'Do you feel all right? You look terrible!'

'Thanks.' Cara gave her a bleary smile.

Pia and Lucie kept her grounded and sane. Even though Cara had changed a lot since they had first met, she needed them more than ever. They were her 'girlie' girlfriends, quite separate from her and Robert's group of peers, who were journalists working in all media. With Pia and Lucie, she could just hang out and talk for the sake of it, without trying hard to impress. If it wasn't for Pia and Lucie, Cara thought, she might be one of those journos who never seemed to go home.

'Party?' Lucie asked, stepping into the kitchen to put the kettle on.

'Not likely,' Pia said, putting her feet up. 'You know Cara's parties – all silver and crystal, candlelight, Brahms and muted conversation. Not dried-up ice-cream on the television screen...'

Cara smiled nervously. Her best friends didn't have to know that she had thrown a carton of ice cream at the television, when Heather Sumner on the evening news had introduced a piece about Dan Hunter's arrival in Australia.

'What happened to you last night?' Lucie set down a tray with a pot of steaming tea, milk and cups.

'Last night?' Cara asked vaguely. She remembered having one of the worst days of her life, then coming home with about fifteen videos and their equal weight in chocolate, and slowly but surely ploughing her way through both.

Pia rolled her eyes.

'We had a date, remember?'

Cara stared straight ahead, and blinked. Pia and Lucie gave each other a meaningful look, and waited as long as they could for Cara to speak. About two-and-a-half seconds.

'Come on, out with it...!'

'You know we can't help unless we know what's going on...'

Cara put up a silencing hand and took a deep breath. After holding out in the face of everything, she was surprised to find her eyes rapidly filling with tears. 'I...I…I've lost my...my...joooooooob!'

Lucie and Pia quickly surrounded her and enveloped her in a group hug, smoothing her hair and murmuring soft words of comfort, and hard words against her boss.

Cara sniffed, gratefully taking the tissue Lucie offered, and mopping at her face.

'Oh, no, Hutch is wonderful really. He's given me every opportunity in the world, and yesterday I acted like an ungrateful cow!'

'Cara, what did you actually *do*?'

'The *Clarion* has been offered an exclusive to tag along with Dan Hunter for a week during the Australian leg of the "Mikhail McHale" tour. He told me to cover it. I refused.'

'You *what*? Dan Hunter is a god! Why would you want to do that?' Pia asked.

'I can't stand the man. And, besides, I'm a serious journalist, which means that I cover the serious issues.'

This last statement did not have the same impact it had had in Hutch's office, the previous day. Not when she was still sniffing tears, her hair was wild, she was lolling around in a prehistoric tracksuit, and her apartment looked like the aftermath of a battle against the forces of chocolate. *This is what he does to me*, she thought. *Whenever his name is mentioned, it's like some sort of incantation, and I'm a dopey kid again.*

Lucie poured a cup of tea and handed it to Cara. 'Come on, you'd never put your career on the line just for that. What's going on?'

Cara took a big gulp of tea, then a big gulp of air. Out the story came, for the first time ever. From her and Dan being born, to being best friends living next door to each other in Davey Street in Toongalla, to promising to marry each other when they grew up, and to the puzzling time in his early teens when he stopped wanting to be with her, closely followed by his merciless teasing.

'Oh, come on,' Pia laughed, 'you mean you're holding a grudge because he used to tease you?'

Cara was deadly serious. 'No. You don't understand.

You know I was an only child, and Dan was everything to me. My friend, my brother...I had no idea why he became so hurtful! I was so confused! He, he...'

In front of her friends, and being honest with herself, she had to admit it. 'He broke my heart.' Cara shook her head. Memories she had denied came flooding back, and with them, a pain that was surprising in its intensity. Again she felt the puzzled hurt, remembered the wet pillow under her young flushed cheek.

'At first, I could insult him as well as he insulted me, but then I began to grow up, and suddenly his barbs really started to sting. You know how insecure you are when you hit puberty. They say he's a comic genius, well, he cut his teeth on me. I was the butt of all his jokes. I was freckly. I was gangly. I was no fun. He used to call me Carrot-top! It was years before I was able to find some confidence in myself!'

'But surely you know how boys are, Cara,' Lucie said gently, 'always teasing the girl they like best?'

Cara violently set her mug on the designer coffee table, spilling tea and not noticing. 'Then, once he was old enough to cotton on to, let's say, *more efficient* ways to show his affection, why didn't he just *stop*?'

That night of the costume ball, he'd known better.

Thinking back on that night for the first time in many years, she tried to regain her sense of indignation, but was shocked to discover the feelings spreading through her now were very much what they'd been fourteen years ago. The sense of hunting, or being hunted, the sensual tenterhooks that she was hanging on, waiting for magic to happen. Heavens above, that kiss...! A naughty, dangerous thought suddenly escaped her. As far as kisses went, *she'd* never known better.

Cara cleared her throat, banishing that last, mutinous

thought with a mental reprimand. *Kisses mean nothing!
You're with Robert for far more important reasons.*

'So, that's it,' Lucie said softly.

'Yep.'

'And it doesn't matter that it was fourteen years ago
and you're now a mature, successful woman,' Pia added.

'Nope.'

The women sat in silence. Cara wished she could
answer differently, but there it was. Unstopping the cork
on the Dan issue also had the unsettling effect of unstopping the cork on a gush of immaturity. Perhaps things
would have been different if she had waited to hear his
explanation. If she didn't keep tuning out her ears and
brain whenever Mum or Denise mentioned him. If only
she and Dan had met as grown-ups. Many 'ifs', but one
fact – this was the way it was. In Cara's mind, Dan only
belonged in one context, and it was that of her childhood.
On an intellectual level, she knew she should look back,
forgive and forget, and even laugh. But on a gut level,
she couldn't. Her gut kept telling her that he should roll
over and die. If losing her job had a plus side, it was that
at least she wouldn't have to spend time with Dan.

Suddenly, Pia jumped up and pulled Cara to her feet.

'You need cheering up,' she said. 'We're going out!'

Lucie was more alchemist than professional chef,
Cara often said, and once again proved it by pulling
together a picnic lunch in record time that could have
fallen out of the pages of *Vogue Entertaining*. Pia
couldn't boil water, let alone cook, but she did know how
to shop, and after dashing next door to her apartment,
she returned with a superb selection of various cheeses
and two bottles of wine.

'Some fresh country air, good food, good wine, and
you'll be good as new,' Lucie said, bundling Cara into
the driver's seat of her Audi.

'Right!' Pia exclaimed. 'Drive on!'

Cara drove on. For about two metres. There was a screech, a jolt, and then a sickening crunch. The women screamed. Shocked, they sat eyes wide open, not quite able to move or speak.

'Cara, are you OK?' Lucie finally asked.

'Uh-huh. Are you OK?

'Yes. Pia, are you OK?'

'Yes, but what happened?'

Cara looked wildly around. What the heck *had* she hit? She couldn't see anything. Quickly, she regained composure and opened the door. Then she saw it – a sports car, classic looking, with only three wheels. Its nose looked decidedly out of joint.

'What is this?' Cara asked. 'Are cars allowed to have three wheels? Or did I just knock one off?'

The other driver was unfolding himself out of the car, adjusting his glasses then, seeing the damage, shaking his head in disbelief.

Cara jogged up to the man, who had now taken his glasses off and had his eyes closed, pinching the bridge of his nose.

'Sir, are you OK? I'm so sorry!'

Instantly the man snapped into action. He pointed a finger at Cara.

'It was your fault! You are the one supposed to give way when you're coming out of a parking space!'

'I didn't see you...! I'm sure my insurance will cover it...'

The man snorted. 'It might cover *some* of it. You've hit my Morgan! A car built the old-fashioned way!'

Cara smiled, trying to lighten the man's increasingly hysterical tone.

'Well, what's the old-fashioned way? By hand?'

'Yes!'

'Oh.'

'Do you have any idea how long it'll take to get the parts, and how much it'll cost?'

'H-how much could it possibly be?' Cara stammered. The man told her.

Cara's eyes and mouth opened in shock. If only the ground would just open up and swallow her.

Cara was calm now.

She had cried. She had screamed at Pia and Lucie for convincing her to drive when she was so upset. She had paced and wrung her hands. She'd had a shower, and with her industrial-strength blow-drier, had straightened her hair to match the sanity she needed to feel. Then she reviewed her options. She didn't like them. But she repeated the words like a mantra, over and over again, as she picked up the phone and dialled Hutch's number… 'Freelancer rates, freelancer rates, freelancer rates…'

A lesser journalist would think Dan Hunter had some nerve. Already, Cara had waited two hours, and had been interrogated by Dan's publicist, his secretary, his body-guard-cum-trainer, and – she thought – his accountant. She breathed into her diaphragm, each breath flooding her body with calm, filling her soul with peace and good-will. She had discovered that mantras helped a lot. They had certainly worked when she told Hutch why she needed the assignment, and he had laughed so hard he nearly choked to death on his barbecued calamari. Her new mantra, 'I am here to do my job, and I will do it well. I am a professional, and so is Dan Hunter. We are now two mature adults and our past has no bearing on this moment…'

'Mr Hunter will see you now,' said Anna Di Vito,

Dan's publicist, suddenly appearing in her field of vision.

Cara smiled graciously and stood up. She smoothed her skirt and jacket, and put a hand to her hair – it was as smooth and shiny as a seal's. She looked good, she felt calm, she had fresh batteries in her tape recorder, and her pencils were sharp. She followed Anna Di Vito into the suite. But even before she could spot him in that room full of hangers-on, she heard him.

'Well, hello there, Carrot-top.'

chapter two

Well, well, well, thought Dan Hunter. Here she was, after all this time, and after all the trouble he had taken to get her here, he had to admit...well, nothing, really. His brain could only come up with one word that it repeated over and over again, bouncing it around the walls of his suddenly mushy cranium. Wow. Wow, wow, wow. And his body was responding to her mere presence in the room far more eloquently than he ever could. Little fishes were swimming up and down his spine, his palms were sweaty, and his pounding heart threatened to leap up his throat and do the talking for him. But he had to say something, right? Something, anything. And before he knew it, it was out.

'Well, hello there, Carrot-top.'

Dan saw her stiffen, and her chin lifted up regally. What a hothead. He wished he hadn't called her that but, still, it was only a childhood nickname. So, he guessed, things weren't so different after all.

Come on! he scolded himself. *What did you expect? That she'd see you, leap into your arms, and tell you how clever and gorgeous and sexy you are, and promise undying love and devotion forever? Well, yes*, he admitted. Maybe he had. But no matter, he resolved, it might take more time, but he'd do it. No matter the trouble, no matter the cost.

'Hello Dan,' Cara said, extending her hand toward him so resolutely that he had no chance to get close enough to give her a peck on the cheek. Her grip was rock-hard, her gaze ice-cool. Where was the wild spark he had seen in her eyes at the costume ball?

'It's been a long time,' he said, softly.

'Mmm...yes,' she said, delicately frowning her brow. 'It must be, what, five, seven years?'

'Fourteen.'

'Fourteen? As long as all that?'

He smiled. Hutch was right about her stubborn streak. But he was happy, just so long as she was there.

Anna Di Vito strode up to them.

'Ms St John, you have time for a twenty-minute preliminary interview. Mr Hunter has other commitments in a half-hour, and you will then have to make your observations without consulting him in any way...'

It was a few moments before Dan could snap out of his shock at Anna's tone.

'Umm...Ms Di Vito, could I speak to you for a moment?' He took her arm and discreetly took her aside. 'Ms Di Vito…'

'Anna, please, Mr Hunter.'

'Anna. I know you're a professional and the studio holds you in high regard, and I wouldn't want to tell you how to do your job...'

'But?' she raised an eyebrow.

'But wouldn't one of the first things they teach you in publicist school be "Don't alienate the journalist"?'

'With all due respect, Mr Hunter, in exactly twenty-nine minutes there's the photo shoot for *Today* magazine, and if she is a professional, she will understand the demands on the time of a man such as yourself.'

'Well, Anna, she is a professional, but can we please take a more "softly, softly" approach? You see, in Australia, we have something known as "the tall poppy syndrome". Ever heard of it?'

Anna shook her head.

'These are all the poppies in the field,' he said, wiggling the fingers of one hand. 'And this…' – his other hand pushed above the other – 'is the poppy that grows above them. Do you know what happens to the tall poppy?'

Anna shook her head once more.

'The grower comes along and…wham!…he cuts the tall poppy down.'

'I see.' Anna nodded thoughtfully, then wrote on her clipboard, 'Tall poppy syndrome. Check.'

'Besides, Cara St John and I go way back, and…'

Anna looked up from her clipboard, frowning. 'You mean you have a history with Ms St John?'

Dan shoved his hands into his pockets. 'Well, what does "history" really mean? I mean, if you're talking about knowing each other in the past, and maybe being involved, or well – maybe not "involved" involved, but, you know, involved…yeah.'

'This could be very awkward,' Anna sighed. 'In my business, I'm used to all the back-scratching that goes on, and I have to admit to knowing about a few one-night stands between the journalist and the interviewee, but I've never heard of the journalist actually being the interviewee's ex-lover.'

'Well, that's all right then,' Dan smiled. 'She's not my ex-lover.'

'Oh. Ex-girlfriend?'

'No.'

'So she's got no gripes against you?'

Dan swallowed hard and fought to keep the smile on his face. 'N-no.'

'And that "tall poppy syndrome" wasn't something you made up just to keep me off Ms St John's case?'

'Definitely not.'

'Fine.' Anna gave Dan a businesslike smile. 'I think we understand each other.'

'I am so glad.' Dan gave her a dazzling smile and turned to his real quarry, Cara.

'Finished consulting?' Cara asked, still standing perfectly poised, exactly where he had left her.

'Yes. Let's take a seat, shall we?'

Dan led Cara to a corner of the sitting room, where two chairs had been set up near the window, showing the glory of the sea beyond. He watched her unpack her materials, wanting to drink her in with his eyes...

'Ready to be measured for that suit?' a voice directly beside his ear asked. It was Scott, his secretary.

'What?'

'Reception just buzzed. They said that the tailor's downstairs.'

'Look!' he yelled. How was he supposed to have time alone with Cara when the studio had lumbered him with a real live entourage? Scott was different. He was his secretary and friend since his stand-up days, and he wouldn't want to do without him, but this was his first Cara sighting in fourteen years! Dan closed his eyes, clenched his fists, and steered his tone into calm waters. It was his own stupid fault for not telling Scott why Cara was here in the first place. He'd do it later – and have someone else on his side. 'I'm sorry, Scott. I'd like to have some privacy for this interview, OK? Could you please get rid of everyone?'

Scott smiled and clapped a hand on Dan's shoulder. 'Sure. OK, everybody, vamoose!'

Scott cleared the room, but not Cara's determination.

'So, Dan, why go back to the Cold War during the eighties for "Mikhail McHale"? Is the espionage genre dead in the 2000's?'

Dan spurted out a chuckle. 'Whoa, whoa! What sort of a first question is that? How about a few light ones to get me warmed up? You know: where I was born, where

I was educated, what my first gig was – that sort of thing.'

'I'm a professional, Dan. I've done my research. I'm not going to waste time asking you things everyone knows already. Besides, you offered the *Clarion* an exclusive, and if I don't provide some exclusive information, my editor's going to have my head on a platter.'

'Exclusive information, eh?' Dan scratched at the golden stubble on his chin. 'All right, how about if you ask me how many times I rang your house after you ran away from me at the formal?'

Cara opened her eyes wide, and sucked all the air out of the room. 'Really! Dan, I…'

'Four times a day for one week. Next question. How many girlfriends have I had since I left Australia?'

'I don't think…'

'I've lost count. How many of them do I remember?'

'Please, this is not…'

'None of them. How many of them was I serious about?'

Cara gripped the armrest of her seat as if it was about to buck her off. 'Right,' she said. 'Do tell, Mr Hunter. How many of them?'

'None of them.' Dan lowered his tone to a soft caress. 'Ask me who I have loved with all my heart ever since I can remember.' Dan prised her hands from the armrests, and gently stroked their creamy skin. 'Please, Cara, ask. Just ask.'

Cara swallowed, looked down, and shook her head, pulling her hands from his. 'Please, Dan. This is not appropriate. I was sent here to do a job, and I intend to do it properly. If you compromise my objectivity, the paper will have to send another journalist.'

Dan sighed, then leaned back against his chair. 'Right. I'm sorry.' He paused. 'OK, I'm ready. Fire away.'

'Why go back to the Cold War during the eighties...?'

Cara had managed a time-out from the interview and locked herself in the bathroom. She braced herself against the sink. The reflection in the mirror was telling her to snap out of it, but the real 3-D Cara couldn't. If this was what she was like after only twenty minutes with Dan – even after a fourteen-year separation – what would she be like after a week?

'Come on!' the reflection in the mirror seemed to say. 'You were there when the Berlin wall came down. You were in the Pacific when the French were testing nuclear devices. You were at the Pauline Hanson assassination attempt. Twenty minutes alone in a room with Dan Hunter is peanuts!'

If this is peanuts, Cara thought, then she was having a real anxiety attack. Why couldn't she stop shaking? Or wanting to melt into an insignificant puddle at the sight of Dan? And most disconcerting of all – this feeling that all her adult life had led up to that one moment when he took her hands and said 'Just ask'?

'Right,' the Cara in the mirror seemed to say, 'Facts are your best friends. What are the facts about what Dan said and your reaction to it? Firstly, Dan's been out of your life for fourteen years. And, before that, he made life unbearable for you. As a matter of fact, the last time you saw him, he absolutely humiliated you. Secondly, you haven't thought about Dan for fourteen years. Not much, anyway. And certainly not in any romantic light. Therefore, if Dan was to tell you he loves you, what are the chances of him meaning it? None. And what are the chances of you wanting to hear him say it? None. If you're antsy, chalk it up to experience. This is what happens when someone tries to compromise your professional integrity.'

Cara turned on the tap and lightly splashed cold water on her face, then patted it dry and repaired her make-up.

A bit of liquid face powder.

No doubt about it, Dan had become a better actor than she had thought.

A little smudged eyeliner.

How many women he had used those lines on? And how many of them had fallen for them? That had been some performance, his rate of success must be pretty impressive.

A little blusher and lipstick.

Obviously, since his first attempt hadn't worked, she had to keep alert. What next? An offer to be in his next movie? Cara stifled a giggle.

Luckily, in her profession, all she had to worry about putting to bed was the paper.

Dan Hunter paced the hotel suite. At any moment, everyone would come barging back in and whisk him away for the photo shoot, and he'd got nowhere with Cara!

There was a brief moment when he thought he'd actually touched her, but no. She wasn't just stubborn, she was also a really cool customer. She'd shut him up about one subject – what he really wanted to talk about – and got him started on the next – what he didn't care about – without so much as batting one of her fair eyelashes! And she was good at what she did. Intelligent questions. He had to admit she really *had* done her homework. Cara smiled encouragingly in the appropriate places, laughed politely when called for, and looked refreshingly interested instead of the usual fawning.

But no matter how pleasant she was, or how many insightful answers she drew from him, the entire time they talked, it felt like there was a force field between them.

Dan put his head against the windowpane, and immediately a shrill cry rose up from the small crowd of girls below, as they screamed themselves into a frenzy of vocal chords. He waved and tried to hide his grimace under a smile. Although he appreciated his fans, and had already spent time with these girls signing autographs and posing for pictures, he didn't understand this sort of adulation, not for a regular bloke from an Aussie country town. The irony of being up on the tenth floor with all those adoring females below wasn't lost on him, particularly when the one woman he wanted was right here, probably wishing she was somewhere else.

You'd think I'd be used to this sort of thing by now, he thought. But the truth was that he wasn't.

He had to admit that, years ago, when he set out for Hollywood with a few thousand dollars and a backpack full of dreams, lots of gorgeous California girls were high on his wish list. He had been 26-years-old, and any self-respecting heterosexual male fame-fantasy had to have girls in it. So he hadn't exactly kept himself celibate, but…supply far exceeded demand. Since his success, he questioned why women were forever throwing themselves at him – like the pneumatic blonde who had turned up earlier pretending to be room service and then presented all her bare assets on a figurative platter. These women – who did they think they saw?

Not me, that's for sure, he thought wryly.

It left him feeling empty inside, like in that Beatles' song, about going out and breaking hearts all around the world, but crying instead. There was only one girl – no, she was a woman now – he wanted. And he had waited long enough.

The bathroom door opened and Cara emerged,

looking refreshed and prim in her navy trouser suit. *Now, if only she had presented herself the way that blonde had...* He cleared his throat. These weren't thoughts he should be entertaining just before a revealing photo shoot.

But maybe there was a little time to spend alone together before the gang came back...

'OK everybody, come right in,' Scott said, opening the door.

'Mr Hunter, I'd like you to meet the photographer from *Today*, Lyn Berkowitz,' said Anna, leading the charge. 'Would you mind moving right out of the way? Thanks, dear.' This last comment was aimed at Cara, who raised her eyebrows and moved further and further backwards until she was tightly wedged in a corner.

OK, OK, I give up, thought Dan. *If they want my body, they can have it.* An assortment of stylists, make-up artists, and hairdressers descended on him, and he let them do what they wanted. His mind was elsewhere. His mind had kidnapped Cara, and they were now speeding away from the hotel in a fast car, towards peace, and solitude, and happy-ever-after-ness.

Phew.

Cara slumped on to the sofa, eased off her shoes, and leaned back. With gentle fingers, she massaged her temples and closed her eyes. No chocolate or rösti today, she vowed. She was going to deal with her stress over Dan the healthy way, or she would wreck her digestive system and balloon up past 'voluptuous' and 'curvaceous'.

No doubt about it, seeing Dan, being with him, had knocked the wind right out of her.

What was it? She supposed it was final confirmation of how she really felt. Before she saw him, she might have conceded – just maybe – that through the years she had added layers to the original hurt, making too much of something that had happened long ago when they were only kids, doing the things kids do. But now, it was real.

She had faced the monster – albeit a dazzling, charming, golden boy of a monster –and found her reaction echoed her every reservation. The pounding heart, the feeling of being out-of-control, even wanting to weep for the moment when he took her hands, it all pointed to the fact that the two of them belonged on separate continents. The sooner she could get this assignment over and done with, the better.

Still, there was a little niggly something that nibbled at the edge of her conscience like a mouse nibbling at cheese on a mousetrap. Careful, careful now, or the trap might snap.

Nibble, nibble.

She knew what it was.

It was that feeling when he held her hands, that feeling of arriving, her weary heart expelling a long-pent-up sigh. As if she had waited all her life for this one moment when this one person would tell her he loved her.

Nibble, nibble.

It was looking into Dan's eyes. His eyes weren't just deep blue, they were deep. As if she could really look into him by looking into his eyes, just like every cliché in every soppy love story. His eyes were like pure water, so clean and free of artifice, so full of...honesty. As if...as if...he'd actually *meant* it.

Snap!

Cara jumped out of her seat as if the sofa had bitten her bottom. She began pacing.

A little voice she had never heard before spoke up inside her head. 'What if Dan really did mean it?'

Obviously this little voice belonged to some other, insane person. Maybe she could reason with it.

He couldn't have.

'Why not?'

Because.

'Oh, that's great reasoning from a seasoned, intelligent journalist!'

Hmm, she thought, *the voice was getting bolder.*

Because...people just don't do *that. They don't spend their time tormenting the person they love, then break contact for fourteen years, and pine for them all that time.*

'They do if they're young. They do if they're frightened of rejection.'

Ha, that's pretty funny. There's not an insecure bone in Dan's body.

'And how would you know? The last time you were interested in Dan's bones – actually jumping them, if I recall correctly – was a very long time ago.'

OK, point taken. Still, this is a non-issue, so why bother me with it? Dan doesn't love me, and he never did.

This time, the voice seemed sad. 'Oh, Cara. Why are you so afraid to believe that Dan loves you?'

chapter three

'Well, if you're not interested in how to look for him, why have you been standing in front of the wardrobe for ten minutes?' Still in her pyjamas, Pia nursed her morning cup of tea, enjoying the rare sight of Cara still in her robe, just fifteen minutes before she usually left for work.

'It has *not* been ten minutes.' Cara didn't bother stopping her intense scrutiny of the neat lines of clothes, shoes, and accessories. 'Isn't there anything colourful in this wardrobe?'

'How can you say that?' Pia asked innocently, taking hangers from the racks. 'Look at the pretty colours! Black suits. They'll make you stand out from the crowd, won't they? Hang on, here's a change of pace! Grey suits. And – Ooh! You wild thing, this is a surprise! – a brown suit!'

Cara turned and glared at her. 'You do know that sarcasm is the lowest form of wit, don't you?'

Pia smiled sweetly. 'Know it? I rely on it! By the way,' she said, putting a brimmed hat on her head, 'I wonder what Rob would say if he could see you like this now, hmm?'

Cara's brow creased. 'If he could see me like what now?'

'You know. Indecisive. Fussing over your appearance. For another man.'

'OK, OK, OK,' Cara put up a halting hand. 'I know where you're heading with this. Firstly, I am not indecisive…'

'Which is why you've been standing in front of this wardrobe for ten minutes.'

'It has *not* been ten minutes! Besides, it's not fussing, and it's not "for a man". I'm merely getting ready to go to work, and I want to look my best. I am not out to impress the interviewee, you know. I am, after all…'

'…a professional. Yes, I know. Is that why you're wearing stockings and a bright red suspender belt?'

Cara started, and wrapped the dressing gown tighter around her body.

'Too late,' Pia chuckled. 'I already saw it. What is it you're going to tell me now? That you're wearing it for *yourself*? That's an oldie, and a goodie.'

'Fine, have it your way.' Cara shrugged with what she hoped was nonchalance. 'But I'll have you remember that I'm not sexless, you know. I *am* in a relationship…'

'Glad you remembered!'

'What's that supposed to mean?'

'Only that Rob hasn't come up in conversation since last Saturday, and it wouldn't surprise me if he hadn't been on your mind at all during that time, either.'

Cara bit her lip. She was about to argue, but she had to concede that Pia was right. She had barely thought about Robert all week! Plain old-fashioned stress, she concluded. She had gone from nearly losing her job to having it absorb her every waking moment, and that sort of thing didn't happen without some sort of casualty. In this case, it had been Robert. Thankfully, if anyone understood the demands of the job, Robert did. They both knew they could always pick up where they left off.

'Robert and I don't have that sort of relationship. We're not kids, we don't have to be hanging on to each other all the time.'

'Yeah, I've noticed. Actually, I've been meaning to

ask for a very long time,' Pia narrowed her eyes, 'just what is the "sort of relationship" you two have?'

Cara sighed and smiled indulgently. 'We're two mature adults. We respect each other, we enjoy each other's company on occasion...'

'Hmm, sounds familiar. I know! I have the same relationship with my accountant.'

'Look Pia, I don't analyse your habit of falling in lust with anything with an XY chromosome, do I? Do you really want to know, or is this just another one of the many times you want to poke fun at me?'

Pia cast her eyes down, chastened. 'Sorry. Really, I'm dying to know.'

'Well, at this stage of my life, I don't want my hormones dictating the sort of man I get involved with. I respect Robert immensely. He has taught me so much – and still does.' *Even if the teaching sometimes involved being brought down a peg or two, she thought, like a couple of weeks ago when he read one of my articles out loud and picked it apart...in front of all our dinner guests.* He was tough sometimes, but she was a better journalist for it. 'We go to the theatre, the opera, the ballet, and sometimes...we spend the night together, which is nice.'

'*Nice*?' Pia looked incredulous.

'Yes, Pia, believe it or not, sex is not the be-all and end-all, you know.' Pia looked away and muttered something under her breath, but she continued. 'And best of all, there are no strings attached. We have complete freedom.'

Pia laughed. 'Complete freedom? No such thing. I mean, couples *talk* about giving each other complete freedom, but that snake always turns around and bites these self-deluded people right in the bum.'

'Well,' Cara sniffed, 'I can see how it would happen

if one of them was bullied into it, but it just so happens that both Robert and I agree. A permanent monogamous relationship – marriage, kids – is an impossible, bourgeois ideal.'

'An impossible, bourgeois ideal? They're strange words for someone whose parents can still be found necking in the car at Lover's Leap on Friday nights. Strange words for a woman who once told me that she wasn't going to settle for less than what her folks have. Strange words for a woman who also said that if her reproductive system was in better shape than her mother's, she'd not only have a kid, but she'd make sure that the kid wasn't an only child. Strange words indeed.' She paused. 'Are you sure they're not Rob's?'

Cara swallowed hard, and lifted her chin. 'People change, and if they're Rob's – I mean Robert's – words, I happen to agree. I have my goals, and I need freedom to pursue them.'

'So you're totally free?'

'Yes.'

'Free to see anyone you want?'

'Yes.'

'And do you?'

'No, but that's not the…'

'And is he free to see anyone he wants?'

'Yes!'

'And does he?'

Cara's face reddened and her eyes and mouth opened, the perfect imitation of a pink bowling ball with red hair! 'Well, I…I…I don't…'

Pia smiled kindly and put her hand on Cara's cheek. 'Sounds to me like a sweet deal. Now,' she said softly, 'would you like to come and pick something out of *my* wardrobe?'

As it happened, Pia's wardrobe was the exact opposite of Cara's. The only suit Pia owned had a skirt shorter than Ally McBeal's, and showed more chest than Hercules. Cara soothed her craving for colour by filching an emerald, sleeveless – backless too, but she intended to keep her jacket on even if it got hot enough for the polar icecaps to melt – turtleneck lycra top, and a violet Thai silk scarf, for one of her black suits.

'Ah, Ms St John.' Anna gave her a tight smile as she opened the door. 'You are on time. Today's schedule, as you can imagine, is packed. First we have an interview with LEO FM, then an appearance on the "Noon Show", then an appearance at "Toyarama" to promote the "Mikhail McHale" action figure…'

Anna's voice melted to a senseless drone as Cara saw Dan, totally unaware and unselfconscious, bent over a sheaf of papers on the desk. He'd been out surfing, like she knew he did every morning, and was wearing nothing but a towel and his beautiful golden skin. His damp, long hair framed his bent head, and his absorbed expression was so boyish that time and surroundings fell away. She knew how his skin would smell – the summery bouquet of salt, sand, sun and sunscreen that, if it could be encapsulated and sold, would make a fortune. Cara knew how that skin would feel and taste too. She remembered the tentative, innocent kisses, the exploratory hands.

Memories of his skin on hers drew her attention back to what she herself was wearing. Red suspender belt, no bra, and…suddenly he looked up directly into her eyes, and the look translated itself into a clear thought that invaded her mind and sent hot feelers through to her very nerve-endings. *He knows what you feel and taste like too*!

If Pia were here, she'd be rolling about on the floor

laughing herself stupid and screaming that she'd known it all along. *Well, I don't think I know anything any more*, Cara told herself as Dan straightened up and walked towards her, his every step turning her heart's tempo and loudness up a notch. She swallowed and fought to bring her heart into some measure of control, telling herself that he was Dan, *Dan*, the man who had made so many of her years needlessly painful.

And yet…she loved to see him. She had said she wasn't sexless, but her nipples didn't come out to say hello to Robert as they were doing now for Dan. Robert wasn't…a product of 'The Land that Reality Forgot!' – she suddenly thought, the justification riding on a cooling wave of relief.

Dan was a movie god. He had been buffed and polished, and had an image tailor-made for him, so that an attraction to him was more than just hoped for. It was manufactured. Robert said that even the most intelligent woman was prey to her rampaging hormones now and then, so why should the curse of hunk appeal bypass her? If normal, intelligent, responsible women could squeal and throw underwear at dancing beefsteaks, then she could be excused for a little warmth in the presence *Today* magazine's, 'Sexiest Man Alive'.

She smiled, in control once more. 'Hello Dan. You didn't have to get dressed up just for me.'

'Neither did you.' He reached up and stroked the scarf, and the warmth of his fingers was so close that the silk might as well have been her skin. 'You know how I love purple. And that green…your mother always used to dress you in green. She said it brought out your eyes.'

Cara's throat dried up. 'I…I did no such thing. I have no idea what colours you like!'

'Don't you?' His dimpled smile sparked his eyes. 'I thought you said you'd done your homework.'

'I did!'

'Then you should know my favourite colours. It's even in the official website…"Dan Hunter loves piña coladas, and getting caught in the rain. He is not into yoga, but is into champagne. *Loves purple and green.*" What sort of a journalist are you?'

Cara sighed. 'OK. Maybe I did know…'

'So you did get dressed up for me!'

Cara glared at his triumphant grin. *Fourteen years, and he's still baiting me, and I'm still falling for it. No matter what I say, I can't win!* Fine, she thought, two can play at this game. She lowered her tone a notch and came closer.

'Well, Dan, you dragged it out of me,' she purred, 'I did get dressed up for you, but this is not all. Do you know what's under this severe black suit?'

Dan's smile changed from playful to something more dangerous. 'Tell me.'

'No bra. Silk stockings, and fire-engine red suspenders…'

'Ahem.'

Cara looked up and there was Anna, foot tapping, face like a gargoyle who's just been called late for dinner.

'Ms St John, your editor told me that you are a professional. Perhaps I misunderstood the kind of professional you are? Maybe I should ring him and find out.'

Cara's face burned with rage and mortification. Not only had she put her professionalism in question, but she had also put the job at risk. If Anna called Hutch and he pulled her out of this job, she'd still be paying her insurance premium when she had her first hip replacement. And what was she supposed to say? 'It's not my fault, Miss! Dan made me do it!' This was exactly the sort of situation that Dan would put her in at school, but the defence didn't suit the self-controlled, mature adult she was now.

'Ha, ha. Busted!' Dan laughed under his breath.

'Shut up!' she hissed through clenched teeth, then smiled pleasantly at Anna. 'Actually, Ms Di Vito, this isn't what it looks like…'

'Oh?' Anna raised one brutally plucked eyebrow.

'No! It's…it's…' She cast a pleading look at Dan.

'Actually, Anna,' Dan smiled affably, 'it's an Australian custom.'

Anna looked suspiciously at Dan, then at Cara, then at Dan, then at Cara, and back at Dan again. 'You're joking, right?'

'No, no!' Cara shook her head earnestly. 'It's called…'

'Coming the uncooked crustacean,' Dan supplied. 'Commonly known as "coming the raw prawn". It's a greeting ritual. Old friends do it when they "come" to see each other. They describe what they're wearing when undressed or, through colloquial corruption, "uncooked". The pink crustacean is symbolic of a white person's colouring when naked, hence…coming the uncooked crustacean!'

Cara looked admiringly at Dan, who looked the picture of authority and trustworthiness. She had to hand it to him, he was quick.

'Is this true?' Anna still looked suspicious.

Cara swallowed hard, smiled through tight lips, and moved her head in a dizzying blend of nodding and shaking side-to-side. 'Hmm, well, yeah…'

'You don't believe us? Hey, Scott!' Dan called out to the next room. 'Would you believe that Cara is wearing a bright red suspender belt under her nun's suit?'

'Oh, don't come the raw prawn!' came the incredulous reply.

'See?' Dan said in all seriousness. 'He doesn't know her very well, and doesn't want to partake in the greeting ritual. Hence "don't come the raw prawn".'

Cara put her hand over her mouth and managed to disguise her rising laughter as a coughing fit.

'Coming the uncooked crustacean,' Anna scribbled in her clipboard. 'Check.'

'Thanks.' Cara smiled at Dan as Anna moved off.

'You're welcome. But tell me…*are* you really wearing a red suspender belt?'

She sighed and put one hand on her hip. 'Really, Dan. What do *you* think?'

Dan looked her up and down and, for the first time in her life, Cara was aware of someone really, truly undressing her with his eyes. She held her breath.

'I guess not,' he sighed as he finished his scrutiny. 'Ah well, it was a nice thought.'

He left Cara standing alone in the middle of the room, mouth agape, dismayed that neither Scott nor he would think she really would wear a red suspender belt.

And doubly dismayed that she should care what Dan thought.

'Just one more stop,' Dan said, catching Cara mid-yawn. 'Then we can call it a day.'

'Sorry. It just slipped out,' Cara smiled crookedly.

The black van – Dan had sent Anna packing when he saw she had booked a limousine – had buzzed like a hyperactive fly from one side of the city to the other, to interviews for television, radio, pay-TV, and magazines, a live appearance at a toy store, and a pre-recorded segment for a comedy show. Cara had tagged along, taking notes and observing. Lots of observing. Never once did Dan complain, mouth off about or to the people who interviewed him, arrive late, or stifle a yawn, as she had just done.

'Ten appointments in eight hours, Dan. How do you do it?' she asked.

'It's business,' Dan shrugged. 'This is a concerted lead-up to the "Mikhail McHale" première tomorrow, and it puts bottoms on seats. Besides, I have an obligation to the people who got me where I am today, you know? Particularly here, in my home country.'

'Obligation? That's a pretty serious word for a comedian. It sounds like a lot of pressure. Don't you get tired?'

'Well,' Dan stretched his long legs in front of him, 'at times it's like what others have said, people don't expect a welder to be welding all the time, and yet they expect a comedian to be funny all the time. Don't get me wrong – I love what I do, but it's not *all* I want to do.'

'Really? You already write, direct, and perform your own material, so what's the next step for someone like you?'

'First, I need to ease up. It's been a frantic seven years, and I need to come home – in more ways than one.'

'What other ways are there to come home?'

Dan smiled softly, but his eyes were intense as he leaned towards her. 'Oh, I think you know the ways. I think you know exactly why I'm here,' he murmured, and ran a finger down her cheek, waking up nerve-endings with an unexpected surge of pleasure. *Coming home*, she thought, and immediately remembered locking herself in the bathroom of Dan's hotel suite, feeling that her entire adult life had been spent waiting for a declaration of love from Dan. He leaned back when he saw her face redden. 'But perhaps it's not something you want to share with your readers.'

His words implied promise, but they sent such a

fearful rush of adrenaline through Cara that they felt like a threat. She searched for words, and the ability to utter them. 'And after you've come home…?' she managed.

'I won't ever totally leave show-business, but I'd like to put some of my other talents to use.'

'Comedian, actor, writer, director – you have other talents?' Cara raised her eyebrows.

'I do, as it happens.' He smiled, keeping his eyes on hers. 'Let me show you.'

All of a sudden, the atmosphere in the van became too close, too intimate. Cara's eyes moved to Dan's long, graceful fingers as they went to the waistband of his black tailored suit trousers. In that split second, her mind went into overdrive, tossing at her mental images that she never meant to see but found unnervingly exciting, of Dan undressing. And undressing for her, holding her eyes in a sensual, intimate gaze, exposing his golden skin for her eyes, hands and mouth to feast on. Cara licked her suddenly dry lips, as if she was already in the grip of a potent craving for something that was yet to come.

Sanity tried to speak up, rather feebly in the light of what Dan seemed to be about to do. *They were in the van! With people up the front!* Sanity cowered off, leaving Cara at the mercy of her burning bloodstream, and her heart went from being merely fluttery to thumping against her chest, like a beast trying to fight its way out as she watched Dan undo the button on his trousers and pull down the zipper.

chapter four

'Dan! What are you?…please, don't do that! S-stop it!'
Cara gasped.

Her face reflected her shock, but she was mesmerized,
and couldn't – wouldn't – look away as he grasped the
waistband and began to pull down. What 'talents' did he
mean? Or did his 'talents' involve…her?

Cara broke out in a cold sweat, which was the result
of the heat coursing through her, lethally combined with
the reality of the situation. Dan's driver-cum-bodyguard
Cory and Anna were up in front but, being Hollywood
types, they were probably used to turning a blind eye to
all sorts of debauchery. She wouldn't be surprised if they
went cruising for girls to bring to Dan's room!

Debauchery with Dan. Some part of her wanted to
laugh. It would have made a great headline except that,
instead of filling her with glee, or even righteous indignation, the idea sent a thrill through her.

Suddenly, Cara's mobile telephone rang. 'H-hello?'
she breathed.

'Hi, Cara. It's me.'

'Me?' she said absently as Dan pulled his trousers
down to reveal silky, touch-me satin in a swirl of colours.
Boxers, she thought. *He wears boxer shorts*.

'Robert.' The voice said pointedly.

'Robert?' The trousers kept coming down and, hey,
these sure were long boxers. '*Robert!*'

'Yeah. Remember me?'

'Don't be silly. Of course I do. How was…?' Long
boxers? No, long trousers! Long satin trousers in wild

colours under his suit trousers? And now he was taking off his jacket and shirt!

'Canberra? Oh – same old, same old. So, tonight. How about it?'

Dan deliberately undid the buttons on his raw silk shirt, still smiling wickedly, still holding her gaze. Then he shrugged the shirt off his pumped shoulders and biceps, uncovering a T-shirt decorated in polka dots, patches, and swirls of glitter.

'How about what?'

'Oh, you know. The usual. A few drinks at Citizen Kane, dinner at Prospero's? We'll take it from there afterwards.'

'Oh! Right.' Dan now took off his fine Italian moccasins, and replaced them with bright yellow Doc Martens with smiley faces all over them. 'It sounds…good. Listen, can I get back to you later? I'm still working.'

'Oh. I thought you were out of the office.'

'I'm in the middle of an interview.' She frowned as Dan brushed his hair back, tied it into a ponytail, and pinned it up. *What the*…?

'You are? Sorry, Cara. Hope it's no one important!'

'No, it's…' Dan put a wig of multicoloured dreadlocks on his head. 'It's…' Then he put a big, red foam nose over his own. He sat back, crossed his arms, and grinned. Robert had all her attention now. 'It's just some clown.'

The van stopped just as Cara hung up.

'Here we are!' Dan said, launching himself out of the van.

Cara registered that they were at Brisbane Children's Hospital, and hurried to follow as Dan, Anna and Cory disappeared through the sliding doors.

'There's not much time, Mr Hunter,' Anna said. 'We were told you must be out before dinnertime, and I believe the trolleys will be arriving in exactly thirty-two minutes.'

'No worries, Anna, will do.'

Cara half-ran, half-skipped to keep up. 'But…' she panted, 'I thought the visit to the Children's Hospital was tomorrow. The schedule said…'

'That's the official visit.' Dan pumped the elevator button. 'This is the unofficial visit.'

'But – why?'

'Kids aren't stupid, Cara. They know when someone is sincere and when someone thinks of them as a photo opportunity. Tomorrow I'll be here, and we'll smile for the cameras and ask for money, but today, it's just me and the kids getting know each other, without the superstar thing.'

'And this is where your talents are taking you next?' she asked. Cara never would have expected this from Dan.

'Yes. HTICH – Humour Therapy in Children's Hospitals. Heard of it?'

'Yes, I have.' She nodded slowly. 'A colleague did a big write-up about it a few years ago when the "Patch Adams" movie came out.'

'Well, Patch was one of the pioneers, but the concept has taken hold all over the world, with patients young and old. HTICH works solely with children.'

'I remember – my colleague said that the founder had lost a child to leukaemia. What was his name?'

'Alistair Hughes, the original Tich. He recruited me.'

'Tich?'

'It's what we call ourselves – much easier for kids to say than a 'humour therapist in children's hospitals'. HTICH workers are so varied – doctors, nurses, paramedics, therapists, volunteers outside the health system – that we needed an original name that covered us all.'

Cara nodded. 'So what do you do? Just go in, and make the kids laugh?'

'That's the short, simple answer.' Dan watched the numbers in the lift light up in turn. 'Yeah, kids laugh, which lightens a very stressful, often terrifying experience, but it also affects their bodies – boosts immune system, improves breathing, and may even release endorphins. But it's more than that.' The elevator doors opened and he looked down at Cara. 'Tiches help *get stuff out*. Most of the time it's through laughter. But sometimes it's tears, and sometimes it's talking – things the parents or medical staff would never hear.'

Dan waved Anna and Cory towards the ward sitting room. 'Get yourselves a cuppa. I think I'll be OK by myself here.' He winked at Cara. 'You come with me.'

Cara followed as he marched to the desk where a nurse was working, head bowed, over a pile of forms.

'Ahem. Sister in charge around?'

The nurse looked up and visibly started. 'Oh! Oh – Mr Hunter, is it?' Dan nodded and she smiled, extending her hand in greeting. 'I'm Sister Jones – Audrey. We've been expecting you. I can't begin to tell you how excited the children are.' She lowered her voice conspiratorially. 'The staff too, but don't worry. I've told them they're not allowed to squeal when they see you, or ask for autographs.'

'Thanks,' Dan smiled. 'I really just want a low-key visit with the kids today. But I could bring some autographed glossies tomorrow.'

Audrey glowed approvingly. 'I'm sure they'd love that. Now – if you'll just follow me…'

'Excuse me,' Cara asked Audrey when she noted a total absence of plaster casts and traction machines. 'What sort of ward is this?'

'I'm sorry, dear, didn't you know?' she smiled. 'It's the cancer ward.'

Cara was thrown for a loop. She had expected a day full of superficiality and gloss, and she'd got it too – until now. If this morning someone had told her that she would be spending the half-hour before dinner in the company of kids with cancer, she would have laughed…and told them not to 'come the raw prawn'. It was unexpected – and maddening! *How dare Dan not prepare me for this!* she thought. *How dare he…how dare he have hidden depths!*

'Are you OK with this, Carrot-top?' he smiled. The old nickname was surprisingly inoffensive coming from a man in multicoloured dreadlocks. He was still the clown, she thought. Nothing changes…and everything changes.

'Sure.'

'Righto. Here we go.'

Dan had a bottle of bubble mixture and, standing outside the door, gently blew bubbles into the room. There were delighted gasps and giggles, and Dan looked back at Cara, smiling with such sweetness that her own heart leapt.

'Can I come in?' he asked, poking his head into the room. There was a soft welcoming chorus, and Dan pulled on Cara's arm. 'Come on, we're on.'

'What do you mean, "we"? There's no "we"…!' she protested, leaning her weight back.

'Damn, you're strong!' He groaned. 'I need help.'

'But, I don't know how…!'

'Cara, will you just lighten up for once in your life and *play along*…!' With a final mighty heave, he managed to unbalance Cara, and they both stumbled into the room, to the delight of the children within.

'Ah, hello everyone! I am Doody, the hospital

hairdresser, and this is my assistant, Carrot-top. Say hello, Carrot-top.'

'H-hello.' For some reason, the children found her shyness funny, and they giggled as she wiggled her fingers in greeting.

'Now,' Dan continued in businesslike tones, 'as you may have heard, if you've been in hospital for longer than one hour, you are entitled to a free haircut. How many of you have been in hospital longer than one hour?'

The children all put up their hands.

'Right! What do you all think, would you like a haircut like mine – or like Carrot-top's here?' There was a chorus of giggled 'nooooooo's and 'yeeeeees's'. 'OK, then. Now – where did I put my scissors…?' Dan shoved his hands down his trousers, rummaging until his arms were in as far as his shoulder. 'That's not it…that's not it…nope, that's not it, either… Woo! That tickles! Aha!'

With that, Dan pulled out a pair of plastic scissors as long as his leg. For a split second the children looked on in shock, then released it with a cacophony of squeals, screams, and laughter. He purposefully strode towards a little boy hooked up to a drip, and there was nothing for it but for Cara to join in.

'No, Doody, you can't!' she exclaimed, restraining him.

'Just a little trim with these here trimming scissors! And if anyone needs a proper haircut, I can go and get my BIG scissors…!'

'No!'

'Oh, come on, don't be a spoilsport…'

They kept going until Dan, in touch with his audience, decided it was time to move on. 'Mingle,' he mouthed to Cara as he began to talk and play with each child individually.

But Cara couldn't mingle. Not yet, anyway. She retreated to a corner and watched, and if she could have seen the goofy smile on her face, she would have been mortified. He had a definite rapport with the children, which was hardly surprising for a man who had been raised in a family of nine children. Despite his silly get-up, he spoke to the children on their level, and she was amazed at how they opened up to him and laughed with him, and sometimes just hugged him without saying a word. There was something warm and precious in the atmosphere that she couldn't put into words, and she wondered how she would write about it. But she could imagine that the fans would love to read about this. Writing that Dan Hunter was good with kids could just about guarantee a cyclone as women around the world heaved a collective, heartfelt sigh.

Was it possible that women nowadays were no longer interested in men who 'gave' them children but shared in them? Making a mental note of this thought as a possible angle for the article, she suddenly realised that looking at Dan and a little boy hugging, she had a tightness in her chest. The kind of tightness that's only eased through…sighing! Just then, Dan looked up, straight into her face, and gave her a gentle smile and a wink. She blushed at being sprung in the middle of her scrutiny, but still, she couldn't look away.

It was many years since she had been with children. Pia and Lucie had none, and she and Robert's social group either had none, or left them with spouses and sitters. When you didn't see kids that often, it was easy to forget that, once upon a time, you had wanted them, very much. Before Robert had made her see sense, of course.

Nonetheless, looking at Dan and the children, she couldn't quite pinpoint the 'sense' he had made her see.

She couldn't remember what the actual argument was that had swayed her against having them, but in this room, full of very sick children, it didn't seem to matter. *These children's parents must be going nuts*, she thought. Having children makes people vulnerable in the most raw, overwhelming way, and yet, if she were to ask the parents whether they preferred having sick children, or never having had them come into their lives, she knew what they would say.

I'll never hurt like that, she thought. But the thought, rather than comforting her, left her feeling cold and empty.

'I love your hair.' Cara heard a soft voice at her elbow, and she looked down. It was a girl, about ten-years-old, wearing a bright red beanie. 'It's like mine – when I've got any, that is.'

Cara smiled and crouched down beside the bed. 'It'll grow back.'

'Yeah, I know.' The girl shrugged. 'But seeing your hair just made me wish – my mum says it's OK to wish.'

'Of course it is. If you don't make wishes, how can any of them come true?'

The girl smiled, holding up a well-loved book. 'That's exactly what the girl in this book says! Fiamma – she's got red hair too.'

Cara saw the title, 'Fiamma and the Unicorn's Bridle', and the familiar name on the cover. She bit her lip. When confronted with the spectre of James St John the children's book author, she usually ignored it and hoped it would go away. It wasn't anything she ever brought up in conversation, and if anyone else ever made the connection, she usually managed to change the subject. But this was different. This girl was actually a fan – a very ill fan who was probably buoyed by the books.

'You like this book?' Cara finally asked.

'Oh yes, I've got all the "Fiamma" books. James St John is my favourite writer.'

'Well,' she whispered, 'can you keep a secret?'

'Yes.' The girl whispered back, nodding gravely.

'James St John is my dad.'

The girl's face split into an amazed grin. 'Really? Truly? Then…then…you are Fiamma!'

'Not really,' Cara laughed. 'But before my Dad started writing, he used to tell me bedtime stories about a plucky little girl with long, curly red hair, and her wonderful adventures.'

'But your hair isn't curly now!'

'No – I straighten it every morning.'

'Why would anyone want to do *that*?'

'Well…' Cara searched for appropriate words to tell her. What was she supposed to say? That the curls symbolised a lack of control? That straight hair suited her sophisticated image? No. With sudden clarity, Cara realised it was all…rubbish. She laughed. 'With my mass of curls, I might not fit through the door!'

The girl smiled. 'What's your real name?'

'Cara.'

'I'm Marie.' Suddenly she was serious, and without the smile mounding up the flesh on her cheekbones, Cara realised just how thin she was. 'Cara, would you tell your Dad something for me?'

'Sure. Anything you want.'

'Tell him…that his books make me want to write. I want to be a writer when I grow up.'

'Hmm. OK, I can tell him that, if you want,' Cara said in a slightly disappointed tone. 'But first, tell me, do you write?'

'Yes!' Marie exclaimed. 'I write all the time! Stories mostly, but my Mum and Doctor Phoebe told me to keep a journal too. I can tell my journal anything at all, and it doesn't care if I'm happy or sad or angry or scared.'

'Well then, you know something? You don't need to wait until you're grown-up. If you write, you're already a writer.'

'I am?' Marie's face instantly went from puzzled to proud. 'I am!'

'So, as one writer to another, what would you like to tell my dad?' Cara grinned.

'Tell him that I...*admire* his work. It makes me want to write more, and write better. Tell him I hope he buys my books one day. I'll even autograph them for him.'

'I'll certainly tell him that.'

Marie was silent, but Cara sensed she wasn't finished speaking yet, so she sat in companionable silence, waiting.

'Cara,' she finally said, 'are you a writer too?'

Cara scrunched up her face and pivoted her palms so-so. 'Well...sort of. I'm a journalist.'

'Like – for a newspaper?'

'Yes.'

'You don't get to write make-believe?'

'No.'

Marie screwed up her face. 'Your Dad is James St John, and you don't write make-believe? Why?'

Cara smiled crookedly, and shrugged her shoulders. Marie looked at her thoughtfully, her index finger on her pale lips. Suddenly, she pointed at her, eyes open in real-isation. 'I know! You straighten your hair, and you also straighten yourself! You straighten your writing, and your mind. I bet you hang out with straight people, too, and your house is always really really tidy.'

Precocious little devil. The insight was so accurate and so shocking that Cara could only look at Marie gob-smacked, as she crossed her arms and leaned back

against her pillows, with the self-satisfied smile of a
detective who's cracked a case. A child's face set with
old-soul eyes. And why not? It was a lot of living in a
very short time. But how to reply?

At that instant, she heard the rattle of the dinner trolleys being pushed out of the service lift. Saved by the
dinner bell!

'All right, everyone,' Audrey said. 'You'll be seeing
Doody and Carrot-top again tomorrow, so let's say
goodbye for now.'

The children waved and called out their goodbyes, and
Cara left the room with an unsettling degree of relief.

'Well?' Dan asked, whipping off his foam nose. 'Was
it as bad as what you thought?'

'No, it wasn't...' It wasn't the sickness that had
disconcerted her, it was sharp-as-a-tack Marie! She
smiled up at Dan. 'You were great with them.' He began
to protest, but she put a hand on his arm. 'I mean it, you
really were great.'

He shrugged. 'I enjoy it.'

There was a sudden silence as his eyes rested on her
hand on his arm, and she felt like a child caught with her
hands in the cookie jar because, for all her sincerity while
she'd offered him the compliment, some part of her had
exulted in the firmness of his biceps, had remembered
the strength it only just hinted at. Even fourteen years
ago, he had been strong enough to lift her up as if she
were a rag doll, just so she could be nearer to him, wrapping her legs around his waist...

'Mr Hunter?' Anna suddenly materialised at their side,
and both Dan and Cara jumped slightly. 'Mr Thwaites,
the hospital director, has asked if he can see you before
you go. He looked fairly nervous – I don't think he wants
to go tomorrow cold.'

'Sure.' Dan shrugged.

In the silence that followed as they made their way to Mr Thwaites' office, Dan suddenly murmured, 'So who is this Robert guy that rang you when we were in the van?'

Cara narrowed her eyes, suddenly wary. It didn't matter that he had just gone and made several sick and emotionally drained children very happy, he was still…Dan. She had to be careful.

'I don't see how it's any of your business.'

'Ah,' he nodded knowingly. 'You're sleeping together.'

Cara immediately bit, 'We're not "sleeping together"!'

Dan's eyes sparkled mischievously, and the hint of a grin played with the corners of his mouth. 'You're not? So what's wrong with him?'

'Nothing's wrong with him!'

'Oh. Is it you then?'

He'd done it again. He'd baited her, as usual, and she'd fallen for it, as usual. Cara didn't know whether she was angrier with him for baiting, or with herself for biting. She clenched her fists, putting all her efforts into keeping them from pummelling him.

'There's nothing wrong with either one of us,' she said, deliberately keeping her voice soft so that Anna and Cory wouldn't hear. 'What I meant was that our relationship is far more than "sleeping together".'

Dan chuckled. 'Yeah, I bet.'

'What's that supposed to mean?'

'I think you think your relationship with Robert is intellectual, respectful, insightful – on a higher plane. Like one of those haute cuisine meals you eat for the message behind it rather than for just enjoying the flavours. And sex between you is like…canned peaches and packet custard for dessert afterwards.'

Cara's mouth dropped open. 'How dare you! I...I...'

'Just as I thought,' Dan chuckled again.

'What!'

'All this righteous indignation – you're the type of woman who approaches sex like a Royal Command performance, aren't you? I mean, you don't really know what it's like to get *down and dirty,* do you? Intellectually, you sort of know what it is, but you can never let go enough to actually do it.' Dan's voice was low and discreet, and his face as they passed the hospital staff was affable, as if they were discussing the weather rather than her sex life.

'You superficial rat,' she said in a pleasant *sotto voce* as she smiled at two flower ladies. 'The last time you saw me, I was just a kid, so you are completely unqualified to have an opinion of me as a woman. Besides, after your extended stay in Babylon, I believe you know all too well what getting down and dirty is like. I'd rather think of sex as something special, than as something base and carnal.'

'Well, unlike you, at least I haven't kidded myself that the kind of sex I'm having is the only kind there is. I've always known there was more – with the right woman. With the right woman, even down and dirty is special. So you go on thinking that what you've got with this Robert character is special. Like me, you know there's more, so if it helps drive the emptiness from your heart, go right ahead. Deep inside, you know you can do better.'

'Oh! That's a good one!' she laughed politely as if he had just boom-boomed a punch line. 'And who can I do better with? You?'

He raised a hand in greeting at an orderly vacuuming the floor. 'You know it's me. You've always known it.'

'Wake up and smell the indifference, Dan. You've had

too many people tell you how wonderful you are – it's given you an inflated sense of your importance in the world. And to me. As a matter of fact, whatever I felt for you once, you killed.' She waved her hand as if flicking away a fly.

'Killed?' The look on his face was unreadable.

'Yes, and not only killed, but my experiences with you ensured that I'll always be attracted to your total opposite.'

'I see. So what's my opposite then? A woman?'

'Oh, you'd love that, wouldn't you, just so you could convert me back to being a heterosexual? Nope, sorry to disappoint you, but you cannot convert me back from real men. Robert respects me and I respect him. He is intelligent, mature, and has a sense of what's important in the world. Robert is a real man.'

'Whereas I am…'

'…a fluff merchant. Ah! Here we are,' she beamed as they arrived at the hospital director's door.

They were let in before a narrow-eyed Dan could answer.

'Mr Hunter!' Mr Thwaites boomed as they went in. He had an impressive, side combed pompadour that was meant to hide the fact that the top of his head was totally bald. Poor man! To achieve this extra-ordinary hairdo, the hair on one side of his head would have to be twice as long as Dan's. 'An honour. A great, great pleasure.'

Dan extended his hand. 'Dan, please.'

Mr Thwaites smiled through pale, tight lips. 'Oh – oh, thank you, Mr Hunter. Dan it is, then. An honour. A great, *great* pleasure.'

As Cara was introduced she noticed how sweaty Mr Thwaites' hand was. She laughed silently to herself. This man worked among lifesavers and miracle workers every day, and yet he was nervous about meeting Dan, a mere entertainer.

'I thought you would want to see the trolley before tomorrow. We've put the money you gave the hospital to good use, and with the many extra donations we received, we think we have something that will meet with HTICH's approval. And yours. *Dan.*' Mr Thwaites grasped his hands before him. 'Shall we?'

'Why not?' Dan smiled. 'Let's check it out.'

Cara wondered what kind of 'trolley' they were going to see. The entry for the official visit to the Brisbane Children's Hospital in Dan's itinerary didn't have many details – certainly no mention of a trolley. Mr Thwaites led them to a locked storage room, where hulked a tall rectangular shape covered in a green sheet. He smiled at the group before grabbing a corner of the sheet, and pulling dramatically.

There were nods and murmurs of approval. 'The trolley' turned out to be a double-sided cabinet on wheels, topped with a display section with pull-down glass doors, and storage room below. Inside the display section, there was an incredible range of, well, fun stuff. There were comedy videos featuring everything from 'Abbot and Costello' to 'The Simpsons', and audio tapes of comedians, humorous songs and poetry. There was a huge range of books, as well as bubble mixture, Lego, slinkies, squirt guns, and Groucho Marx noses. Mr Thwaites put on one of the Groucho noses and pretended to hold a cigar beside his face.

'You know, clowns are like aspirin, only they work twice as fast.' He paused, then pulled off the nose and cleared his throat. 'He said that, you know. Groucho Marx. So I'm told. There are more items below. See?'

He unlocked the doors to reveal even more material, including Walkmans and video players.

'It's great,' Dan nodded, impressed. 'Only – what's this?' He pointed to the sign painted on the trolley. It said 'Diversional Therapy'.

Mr Thwaites cleared his throat again. 'Well, the board thought…actually it was Miss Hargreaves, but eventually we all agreed, that the term "Jolly Trolley" did not fit with the mission of the hospital…' His voice trailed off as Dan pulled off his wig, put his hands on his hips, and stared him down.

'Well, Mr Thwaites, I'm not familiar with the mission of the hospital, but am I right in assuming at least some of it involves getting children well?'

'Of course…'

Cara was not surprised by the sweat beading Mr Thwaites' upper lip, or his furtive 'where's the escape hatch' glances around the room. Dan really did look quite formidable, and as his voice dropped a note and rose a decibel, Cara realised everyone was in for a speech of 'Mr Smith Goes to Washington' proportions.

'You're familiar with the research, and I don't need to remind you of all the physiological or psychological benefits of humour on sick people. But let me tell you one thing that you do need reminding about, each and every one of the kids in this hospital is sick of being here. No matter how nice the staff are, no matter how much ice cream they get, it's still a hospital. They're sick of medicine, they're sick of treatment, they're sick of therapy, they're sick of being sick. Even if I was to tell them that laughter is the best medicine, somewhere deep inside they would register the word "medicine", and might subconsciously resent it. When they see this sign saying, "Diversional Therapy", no matter how much they love what's inside, they'll still know it's therapy and, again, there is a very good chance they'll subconsciously resent it so it does them no good. So let's keep the benefits to ourselves, and let the kids have the humour just for fun's sake. I don't care what you call it – "Jolly Trolley", "Cackle Cart", "Laughs on Wheels", "Mobile Humour", whatever – just leave the jargon out of it.'

'I understand your point, Dan, but Miss Hargreaves…'

'Aha!' Dan nodded. 'So she's the troublemaker, is she?' Mr Thwaites looked down but was silent. 'Come on, you can tell us. The board was OK with the term "Jolly Trolley" but it was this Miss Hargreaves who dug her heels in? A simple nod or shake of the head will do, Mr Thwaites.'

Mr Thwaites nodded.

'Well,' Dan clapped his hands together and rubbed them. 'In that case, I know exactly what to do. Anna?'

Anna smiled at Dan, the kind of smile you could imagine on a piranha after you asked it what it felt like for dessert. 'She sounds like a fascinating woman. I look forward to meeting her.'

Cara looked from Dan to Anna and back to Dan incredulously. Jeez! She had always thought that Anna Di Vito was pretty frightening, but she hadn't imagined that Dan would actually put her on to people! She had no idea what Anna and Dan had in mind for poor Miss Hargreaves, but she made a mental note of the time and date, just in case the police came around asking why a little old woman had been found hanging upside down from scaffolding somewhere!

'That was pretty impressive, what you did back there,' Cara said to Dan as they climbed into the back of the van, and Anna and Cory settled themselves up front.

'What – getting the name changed back to "Jolly Trolley"?' Cara nodded, and Dan smiled. 'Yeah, I thought so.'

Putting his shirt back on, Dan seemed quite affable

now that Anna was going to convince Miss Hargreaves that naming the facility a 'Jolly Trolley' was better than…oh, she didn't want to think about what Anna would threaten her with.

'You really are used to getting your own way now that you are a star, aren't you?'

Dan stopped mid-button and became serious. It wasn't that different a look from the one that had made Mr Thwaites break out in a sweat. 'What do you mean?'

'In a word? Star status.'

'That's two words.'

'Whatever. It gets you a table in a booked-out restaurant, or an on-site trailer fitted out like an oil magnate's yacht. And if you don't get what you want, you…do your lolly.'

'Do my lolly? Do my *lolly*?' Dan's voice rose.

'It's an Australian expression, Mr Hunter,' Anna interjected from the front. 'Scott bought me a copy of the Dinkum Dictionary. It means…'

'I know what it means!' He glared at Cara. 'Are you implying that I've turned into some sort of …of…*prima donna*?'

'*Primo uomo*, actually,' Anna smiled at Cara in explanation. 'My great-grandparents were from Lombardy.'

'Thank you for the lessons in both the Australian vernacular and Italian, Anna. I can take it from here. Did you ever think,' Dan redirected to Cara in a more discreet tone, 'that I might just be passionate about this? That instead of ego, it's genuine care?'

'Well, don't pretend that you didn't use your status to intimidate…'

'I would have reacted the same if I were a cave-dwelling hermit! Now, answer the question, do you really think that my ego motivated me?'

'Well…'

'Come on – do you?'

The look on his face was deadly serious now, and it seemed like there was more riding on her answer than Cara knew. The truth was, she honestly hadn't thought about him being 'passionate' about HTICH. After all, every celebrity has a pet cause, right? It's good PR. She couldn't lie to him just to feed his ego – particularly when he had spared no thought for her own by passing judgement on her relationship with Robert.

She cleared her throat, the ghost of a smile tugging at a corner of her mouth. 'Well, as a matter of fact, I do.'

As soon as the words were uttered, she knew they had been a mistake. They worked like a magic spell, and everything within the van – seemingly even the engine's drone – stilled to a deadly, cold silence. Dan said nothing. There was no smile, no smart retort. Nothing.

Dan finished dressing, and then sat looking out of the window into the last of the day. He did not talk to her again, and did nothing to deflect the unexpected sense of loss and regret now stealing across her heart.

chapter five

'Where have you been?' Robert gave Cara a quick peck on the cheek and checked his watch. 'We've all been waiting for ages.'

'All? Who's "all"?' she asked, slightly dazed.

'Oh, everyone's here.'

'Are they? I thought we were catching up, just the two of us. Intimately?' she added hopefully, thinking of the red suspender belt going to waste. She looked up at him with what she hoped was a seductive smile but he was already looking left and right to cross the road.

'You did? Why would you think that? I know I never said anything to give you that idea.'

As usual, he was totally right. She could push her point and ask why they had to do duty with the cronies before being alone, but suddenly, there seemed little point. She was tired. She sighed wearily, grasped Robert's arm, and quickly dodged the traffic to the other side of the road.

Cara was still smarting from the effects of her comments to Dan. Since then, she had been alone with her thoughts, and her thoughts hadn't been pretty. They told her that she said what she did not out of honesty, but vindictiveness. Dan had showed no ego in getting rid of the limo, or going to the hospital without cameras present, or using a stage name with the children, or moving about the hospital as if he were staff. She probably would have felt OK if he'd reacted angrily at her comments, but he hadn't. He had actually appeared – was it possible? – *hurt*.

Some part of her had known a lot was riding on her answer. Did she know it was in her power to hurt him? Had she deliberately done it? The thought of being so deliberately sadistic and childish made her feel sick. Sick to the stomach, sick in her heart. Over and over, she saw Dan's face as he looked out of the window, like a light had gone out of it, and she had pulled the switch. The responsibility of it weighed heavy, but if it showed on her face, Robert didn't remark on it.

Inside Citizen Kane, the bar of choice for journalists and assorted media types in Brisbane, Cara and Robert dodged more traffic, human this time, to get to their group's usual table in the private room, which had its own brass-fitted bar and a blazing fire every night of the year, no matter how tropical the temperatures. Their group consisted of journalists from all media, including the *Clarion*, and Robert's paper, the *Antipodean*. Their already boisterous voices rose even higher in a welcoming chorus for Cara and Robert, and they scooted chairs aside to make room.

'So. Bobby, Cara. How have you been?'

The modulated tones, complete with pauses-for-effect, were Heather Sumner's, who sat next to Robert and gave him her best newsreader's smile. Cara remembered Pia's theory – in a party, you can tell a man's mates, because they're calling him Dick; you can tell his wife or partner because she's calling him Richard; and you can tell the one flirting or sleeping with him because she's calling him Dickie. *Oh, Pia would love this*, Cara thought. A perfect example, substituting Bob, Robert, and Bobby. She looked thoughtfully at Heather and the way she smiled at Robert, hanging on his every gospel-like word. She had known Heather at university, and knew that that smile must have cost thousands. How long had Heather been hanging around like this, insinuating herself into their company, pressing close to Robert and laughing throatily at his every witticism? A couple of months at least, she suddenly realised. Marie was right! If she didn't work so hard at 'straightening' herself and being mature all the time, she would have given Heather the boot when she first started trying to elbow in. The thought of Marie, combined with the ever-present image of Dan like a backdrop in her mind, set a match to something brittle and dry like kindling that had been patiently waiting inside her for a long time. With a quick gesture, she signalled the waiter and turned to look at Heather.

'So, Heather, how's the dentist?'

Heather turned, reluctantly, from Robert's holy visage. 'What?'

'You know, that guy you were seeing?'

'You mean the barrister,' Heather said pointedly.

'Barrister, dentist – whatever. Although from what I recall, you were seeing the dentist too. A lot!' she smiled charmingly, then turned to the waiter. 'Frozen chilli vodka. A double.'

'Never mind me!' Heather smiled back, perfect teeth dripping poison. 'What about you? I've heard you've got the hottest date in town for an entire week!'

Robert looked from Heather to Cara. 'What do you mean?'

'Haven't you heard? She's squiring Dan Hunter for the week!'

There was a split second's silence, and then the entire table erupted into hoots of laughter. Robert was laughing too.

'Glad you find it funny,' she muttered through gritted teeth. The vodka arrived and she slammed it back – something every journalist stationed in Russia learns to do – barely flinching at its fire-and-ice sting on the back of her throat and all the way down. She signalled for another.

Robert patted her shoulder. He *patted* her shoulder! 'Oh, come on, Cara. It's not like you to be bitter.'

She shrugged his hand off and brought her face up to his. 'How do you know it's not like me to be bitter? How do you know I'm not the sort of person who will stew and stew over something for years, and then one day, WHAM!' – Robert flinched as she hit her palm with her fist – 'exact my revenge? How do you *know*?'

The second chilli vodka arrived. The first one had anaesthetised her throat, so this one went down even easier, settling comfortably in her tummy and flooding her body with radiating, tingling warmth. This was nice! She signalled to the waiter to bring her the bottle.

Robert chuckled confidently. 'Well, here's what I *do* know. *My* Cara is a serious journalist…'

'Yeah, well,' Cara interrupted, bringing the third vodka to her lips, '*my* Cara needs to earn a crust. And just because you think a topic is light, it doesn't mean that it can't be done well.'

Suddenly, the whole room seemed to be hanging on their conversation. Robert leaned back, his smile indulgent. He had an audience, and he knew it.

'But you see, the "serious" celebrity interview is one of the fallacies of our time. It's an oxymoron! Even when they give the celebrity some sort of pseudo-important, pop culture role, they are still pandering to the publicity machine. When was the last time you read a disparaging interview about a celebrity? It just doesn't happen, because the repercussions for the publication and the media company that owns it, are vast. They're all connected, and they're all scratching each other's backs. You'll see this arty black-and-white photograph of the latest actress to bare her breasts for several million dollars, and the article underneath will say nothing more than, "She bared her goodies for a really valid, socially-aware reason. And if you don't care about her reasons, but you really like her breasts anyway, that's OK, because she's got a genius IQ. What a gal"!'

Cara smiled crookedly. 'Congratulations. Sound argument as usual, Robert, but you're forgetting one thing. The readers love Dan Hunter. No matter what you think of yourself, or what *people*' – she raised her fourth glass to Heather as she said the word – 'tell you about you, you're not above the readers.'

Robert's smile vanished. 'And to appeal to the readers, often you have to appeal to the lowest common denominator. Perhaps, being the daughter of a writer of fairy-tales, you understand this too well.'

There were gasps, and Cara looked at Robert with glittering eyes. He had criticised her work before – always constructively, or so she had thought – but this was a new one. Way below the belt, calling her integrity into question, but also bringing in her dad. No one mentioned her career and her dad's in the same sentence and got away with it.

'And speaking of lowest common denominator, doesn't everyone find it as funny that Dan Hunter has been on the television news – including yours, Heather – every day since he's been here?'

Heather made to speak, but Robert silently put a hand on her arm. It was this final, simple gesture that spoke volumes to Cara. You didn't become spokesman for someone without paying for the privilege with a lot of intimacy. Thanks Marie, thanks frozen chilli vodka, for helping me see things clearly. Shifting loyalties. Shifting beds.

'Well,' Robert said, 'you can't blame Heather for that. She doesn't program the news, or write them.'

Cara smiled and shook her head. 'And you mean to tell me, Bobby darling, that you justify her supposed brand of journalism – no writing, no control over the items, not even any memorising – over my work? Are you sure I'm the only one selling out here?' The corners of Robert's mouth pulled down in anger, but she patted his cheek. 'Oh, I hope she's worth it in bed because, out in the real world, she's as good for your credibility as Dan Hunter is for mine.'

Cara gave him no time to reply. She grabbed her bag and the remains of the bottle of vodka, and strode out.

'Chilli vodka?' Scott said softly as he entered the darkened room. 'You know that stuff will rot your guts.'

Dan sat by the window, the only light that of a dimmed lamp beside him. He looked out to sea, the winking lights of far-away ships crossing his field of vision, thinking of all the clichés that were coming true for him. Ships that pass in the night. Love is like boarding a ship and a-putting to sea. The 'Love Boat' promises something for everyone.

He raised his glass. 'So what's another ulcer? Come and join me.'

Scott sat across from him and poured himself a glass. 'Cara?' Dan nodded, and he sighed as he leaned back. 'So what's happened?'

'I thought it was all going well,' Dan shrugged. 'I mean even when we're sparring, we're great sparring partners, you know? But today I pushed too hard. I went in, guns blazing, and got stuck into her current relationship.'

'What? You mean she's involved?'

'Yeah, with some guy called Robert. I didn't even think she'd be with someone! And I can't believe what an idiot I was! Do you know what I actually told her? That she approaches sex like a Royal Command performance!'

Scott put a hand on his forehead. 'Dan! What are you – nuts?'

'Nuts? Please.' Dan put his hand up. 'You're too kind. I've been calling myself every name in the big black dirty book. But when I heard her talking to him, setting up a date, and then describing me as a clown to him, I don't know…I lost it. Up until then, I thought I was getting Brownie points from her for my Tich work. Then it became clear.'

'What did?'

'She thinks I do it for my ego.'

Scott shrugged and took a slug. 'So? Does it matter why anyone works for a worthy cause? As long as the work gets done?'

'Look,' Dan sighed, 'you know I love the work and, honestly, I don't give a damn why anyone thinks I do it, just as long as they keep supporting us and sending us money. But I do care what *she* thinks. I could make her laugh, I could show her a good time, I could even get her to bed, and it would mean absolutely nothing if she doesn't respect me – at least in some way. If she doesn't respect the comedy, or the movies, that's fair enough. But if she doesn't respect me for this…I don't know. It's my future, it's what I really care about. What's the point in trying any more?'

Scott leaned forward, hands on his thighs. 'Oh, mate! Are you serious? After all this trouble?'

'Well, what else can I do? I don't just want to woo her – I want to marry her! If she doesn't respect me, well, I might as well sign the marriage certificate and the divorce papers at the same time!'

The two men were silent, one staring out of the window, the other staring at the plush carpet.

'Hmm. You say Cara keeps herself under control?'

'Well, it's not just control. It's full on denying that

wild spark she has inside. I know it's still in there somewhere…'

'Then, that's your problem,' Scott concluded. 'If she denies different parts of her personality, why should she accept different parts of yours? To her, your serious streak is as unlikely as her wild streak.'

Dan's eyes opened and his face lit up with a dawning ray of hope. 'You reckon?'

'I reckon.'

'So, if she got in touch with her inner wild child, she might accept…'

'Your mild child?' Scott laughed. 'Well, I'm no shrink, but given what you've already done to get her here, I reckon it's worth a shot.'

'But – how?'

'Well, I don't know really, but right now Cara's on home ground. She's built her life around the way she sees herself. You've got to wonder what would happen if you got Cara away from her preferred environment.'

'But – there's no way I can get her or myself away! Our schedule is totally crazy!'

'Well,' Scott drained his vodka, stood up to leave, and clapped Dan on the back. 'You'll think of something. You always do.'

Dan stared at the clear liquid in his glass. What would be the place furthest away from Cara's preferred environment? Where could he get Cara at a disadvantage? Where could Cara get in touch with her old self? A single name made his morose face break into a grin.

Toongalla!

'Damn you, Dan Hunter!'

Ouch. Cara's head reverberated with the ringing pain of the grandmother of all hangovers, courtesy of the now empty bottle of chilli vodka lying on the floor beside the sofa. Great! She'd gone from chocolate and rösti to heavy liquor in one fell swoop, and all because of *him*.

Ever since he'd arrived, he'd proceeded to take her life apart, bit-by-bit.

First, he had nearly cost her her job. Then, when her job was secure, it was helping him promote his piece of fluff instead of covering the important issues.

Then, he had turned her into a bubblehead whose conversation would not be out of place in the schoolyard.

Then, he had messed with her mind, saying that all this time he had loved her, pined for her, and had actually come home to her.

Then, he had sown the seeds of doubt in her mind about her relationship with Robert.

Then, he had lost her the respect of her peers.

And then, he had blown her relationship with Robert.

All because being around Dan brought out all her insecurity and childishness.

All because she felt guilty.

All because Heather had called Robert, 'Bobby'.

And...do I really approach sex as a Royal Command performance?

Oh, I must be crazy! she chided herself as she punched Robert's number on the telephone. Robert and I have something good and rare – an open, honest relationship. We always said we were free to see other people, that monogamy was an impossible, bourgeois ideal. And, anyway, I probably imagined a thing between Robert and Heather, thanks to that stupid vodka. She kicked the bottle out of sight under the sofa.

'This is Robert Neville. Please leave a message.'

'Robert? Robert, are you home? Please pick up.'

Beep.

Cara sighed, and dialled the number of the *Antipodean*.

'Sorry, Cara, he's not in yet. Would you like to leave a message?'

Cara closed her eyes. 'Umm…could you please tell him that I'm…Oh, just tell him to ring me, would you please?'

'Hmm…' Something inside her said as she hung up. 'Maybe you should try him at Heather's.'

The little psychotic voice. It was back!

Look, you just shut up. Last time we spoke you wanted me to believe Dan was still in love with me.

'Well, isn't he?'

Of course not. He's got an ego as big as Queensland, and just wants my notch on his belt. But it's not going to happen.

'No?'

No! I must apologise to Robert and try to salvage what we had.

'Salvage what, exactly? Being an appendage to a man whose own ego makes him think he has the right to ridicule you in front of your peers?'

Nonsense. Robert has always had my best interest in mind. It's not ridicule, it's constructive criticism.

'Constructive, is it? So how do you feel after it? Built up or demolished? Dan would never put you down like that. And he would never betray you like Robert did.'

Betrayal doesn't come into it. He and I have an understanding.

'Ah, of course, I'm forgetting your part in all of this. The *understanding*! Robert didn't do anything you didn't give him complete and total permission to do, did he? Every time he criticised you, you said, "Oh yes please, Robert, it's for my own good." Every time he took you for granted, you said, "Isn't it good how we can just pick up where we left off?" Every time he sub- stituted one of your goals with one of his own, you said,

"Oh, yes Robert, thank you for letting me see how your way of doing is better." Pathetic, that's what it is.'

That's enough. This is my life, and I know exactly what I'm doing. My relationship with Robert isn't perfect, I know, but that doesn't mean it can't be fixed. Now – why don't you just go back to where you were before Dan showed up?

'All right, sure. I'll get back in the box with all the other stuff you've been avoiding since you were a kid. But, believe me, something in that box will make an appearance sooner or later and, if it isn't me, it'll be something else.'

Cara strode out of the apartment with her shirt hanging out and the buttons on her jacket mismatched. There were things she had been avoiding since she was a child? Other than Dan? Ridiculous! Besides, there was no time for navel gazing because, right now, she had a job to do, and she intended to do it well. Even if her life at the moment appeared to be crumbling beneath her feet, after this job she could set about repairing all the damage Dan had wreaked. And, in the four days remaining, she would ensure that there were no more casualties. Looking at her feet, she almost missed Pia and Lucie as they made their way to her place to catch up on the gossip before breakfast.

'Not so fast,' Pia grabbed Cara's wrist and began pulling her back towards the apartment.

'Nice to see you too, Pia. I'm running late, girls. Can't this wait?'

'No, it can't.' Lucie was quietly firm. 'It will only take a few minutes.' Once in the apartment, she took Cara gently by the arm and led her to the living room.

'Chick flick?' Cara asked when she saw Pia put a videotape into the VCR. 'Shall I microwave some popcorn?'

Pia squinted at the tiny writing on the remote and pressed a button. 'The truth is in here!' she announced as the television blinked on.

The three women sat on the sofa facing the screen. Pia and Lucie, on either side of Cara, turned to look at her face as the words, 'Starring Dan Hunter' faded in and out, then again at 'Written by Dan Hunter'.

'Why would I want to watch this?' Cara thumbed at the screen. 'Mum tried to talk me into going with them to the première, and one time I was visiting, Dad put the video on. Thank heavens the dog needed to go for a walk.'

'Just watch!' Pia said. 'You might learn something.'

'From infantile, puerile trash? I don't think so.' Cara made to get up but was immediately pulled back down by two pairs of surprisingly strong and determined hands. 'Two against one! You don't play fair...!'

'It's for your own good,' Lucie wagged a finger in Cara's face. 'Now sit down, shut up, and watch.'

Cara sat, arms and legs crossed, chin down on her chest, scowling at the action on the screen. So far, she had resisted seeing any of Dan's movies, but she remembered that this was the first one he had made. The humour was so broad it wouldn't have fit into an extra large girdle. It had everything but the kitchen sink. Parodies, slapstick, running gags, stuff happening in the background...and, oh yes, there was a plot in there too. It was the 'School Wild Guy Wins Heart of School Ice Maiden' plot, done to death in the raunchy teen movies of the time. Dan deserved points for trying.

'Does the girl in the story look familiar to you?' Lucie asked.

Cara shrugged. 'Hmm. She does look a little like Nicole Kidman, but I know it's not her. She wouldn't touch this turkey if it were Christmas...'

'Jeez!' Pia threw her hands up in the air. 'How can someone so intelligent be so dumb? Don't you recognise the plot?'

'Yeah, it's old hat...'

'Look! Just look, will you? It's supposed to be you!'

Cara looked at Pia's face, nodding gravely. 'You know I've had my suspicions in the past, but now I know: you really *are* crazy.'

Pia rolled her eyes, and Lucie leaned over and took the remote from her.

'Let's cut to the chase.'

'There's a chase scene? Oh, goody.'

'Shut up, Cara,' her friends said simultaneously.

Lucie fast forwarded, then hit 'play' again.

A school dance.

The 'School Ice Maiden' in Elizabeth I costume eyeing the 'School Wild Guy' who is disguised as Count Dracula.

They dance.

They look into each other's eyes.

They go outside.

Close up of a 'Wet Paint' sign on the fence. A breeze comes up and blows it away.

The 'Ice Maiden' and the 'Wild Guy' move to the fence. Leaning against it, they kiss. The soundtrack saxophone intensifies as her hands move over his chest and shoulders, and he lifts her on to the fence.

The 'Ice Maiden' takes off the 'Wild Guy's' mask.

She slaps him.

She walks away.

There are broad white paint stripes across her bottom.

'Wait!' The 'Wild Guy' calls.

The 'Ice Maiden' – in a rather un-Ice Maiden tone – tells him where to go.

She turns to walk away once more.

He tries to stop her, by stomping on the train of her dress.

The back of the dress rips off, displaying curves and creamy skin, and delicate black lace knickers.

The 'Ice Maiden' walks on, unaware.

Lucie pressed 'Stop'.

'Very funny,' Cara said, looking straight ahead, nodding slowly. 'I can see how audiences would have found that very funny.'

'Cara, are you OK?' Lucie asked.

'Hmm? Yes, why wouldn't I be?'

'You do realise who it was supposed to be now, don't you?' Pia said. 'You and Dan! This changes everything!'

'I have no idea what you're talking about.'

'She's in shock, Lucie, slap her. No, better still, let *me* slap her.'

Lucie took Cara's hands. 'Cara, come on...'

Cara stood up and started pacing in front of the television. 'No! You come on. That girl looks nothing like me. And I never slapped Dan. And I never wore black lace knickers when I was that age! And, and...AND THERE WAS NO "WET PAINT" SIGN!'

Lucie put a gentle hand on Cara's shoulder. 'It's OK. We're not trying to upset you...'

'WHO'S UPSET?'

'You're upset. Calm down a bit and…'

'I *am* calm! I mean, maybe you're the one that's upset and projecting it on to me because any fool can see that that's not supposed to be me and that's not supposed to be Dan. Slapping Dan is something I definitely wanted to do but didn't and, besides, I had half a brain unlike the bimbo in this film who's too stupid to see it was obviously him behind the mask and maybe...'

Cara kept pacing and ranting without drawing breath.

She didn't hear the telephone ring, so Pia shrugged and picked it up.

'...she's too immature to accept responsibility that she pounced on this guy before even considering it might not be 'The School Hunk', and didn't she see him chatting up a girl near the speakers anyway...?'

'Cara...' Pia said.

'I mean the plot holes are so big and black they're sucking in the galaxy and if Dan is so talented, why wouldn't he have seen this, because...'

'CARA!' Pia finally yelled.

'What? What?' Cara said, snapping out of her tirade.

'It's Dan Hunter on the phone. And he says he can hear you in the background, so don't even pretend you're not home. He says he needs you.'

Cara blinked. Once, twice. 'H-Hello?' she breathed into the mouthpiece. Her brain was trying to get a grip on what she had just seen, as well as the fact that Dan was on the telephone.

'Hi,' Dan said. 'That was some diatribe! Did I interrupt something important?'

'Yeah...No! No, you didn't. I was just discussing the merits of this...film.'

'Hmm. Must have been some film.'

'Quite.' She paused. 'Well, Dan, if you're calling because I'm late, I'm sorry. I'm on my way out the door right now.'

'Oh no, that's all right. I'm ringing because I've just been speaking to Mum. She said to remind you about the barbecue in Toongalla on Saturday.'

Toongalla.

Mention of her hometown made something snap back into place in her head, and suddenly she was back to normal.

'Oh, right. Thanks for the call, Dan, but I already told

Mum to tell Denise I couldn't come.'

'Oh.' There was a brief pause on the other end of the line. 'Well, I suppose I'd better get off the line. Anna will want to give Hutch a ring...'

'What? Why?'

'Well, you know Anna. This arrangement for "A Week in the Life of Dan Hunter" with the *Clarion* was her idea. She was absolutely convinced that the best way to round off this leg of the tour was for a newspaper to cover my movements for the entire week. Brian Hutchence is a tough nut to crack, but Anna is very...determined. She made him see things her way in the end. He promised her a week.'

'Well, a working week, weekend excluded.'

'Hang on, let me just ask Anna.' There was a pause as Dan put his hand over the mouthpiece.

Oh, good grief, thought Cara. She needed the money for that wretched Morgan, and here was Dan, threatening to put Anna on to *her*!

'Hello, Cara? Anna says that's just five days. Where she comes from, a week is seven days, and each one's for working. What do I tell her?'

Cara bit her lower lip and closed her eyes. 'Fine. Saturday and Sunday too. I'll be there.'

'I'll tell Mum. She will be pleased,' Dan chuckled.

That marvellous sound flowed, warm and sweet down the line and, as her brain registered it, she remembered what it was about Dan's laugh before he had become her nemesis. It always made Cara laugh, too. Cara smiled, trying to keep the laughter in.

'Dan?'

'Yes?'

'Anna Di Vito's not there, is she?'

'No.'

'See you later, Dan.'

'All right. But you won't be long, right?'

'No!' Cara couldn't help it. A giggle escaped.

'Have a safe drive.'

'I will.'

'Cara? Are you still there?'

'Yes. What is it?'

'Nothing. Just checking.'

'See you later, Dan.' Cara said pointedly.

'Sorry. See you later. You hang up first.'

'Why should I? You hang up first!'

'I can't do that to you, Cara.'

'OK. Bye.'

'Bye.'

'Bye.'

Cara gently replaced the receiver and sighed, smiling to herself. Or rather, she thought she was smiling to herself. Pia and Lucie saw the tender smile and the luminous eyes, and they stared at her. And kept on staring at her.

'What?' asked Cara when she finally saw them staring. 'What!'

chapter six

Cara made her escape before Pia and Lucie could interrogate her. The sheer weirdness of going from being worried to death about her future with Robert, to gazing fondly at the very phone that had delivered Dan's voice, wasn't lost on her. But wasn't weirdness what it was all about when Dan was in her life?

She chewed and chewed over what she had just seen and what it meant. Unlike Pia and Lucie, she doubted that the scene between the 'Ice Maiden' and the 'Wild Guy' was a case of art imitating life. After all, Dan had a history of making life hell for her, not a history of loving her with great, unrequited passion. But that was just one side of the coin anyway. Even if things had happened just as they had in the movie, the truth was that the two of them were separated not just by time and distance, but by emotional and mental galaxies. Now, she and Robert were a different thing altogether. They were one of a kind. They shared the same goals, the same outlook on life.

Or at least, they *had*.

Her stomach lurched painfully. She had to resolve things with Robert. Robert knew who Cara really was. Robert would keep that Cara safe.

Dan answered the door of the hotel room himself. Cara's eyes widened in surprise, then narrowed in suspicion as she saw that they were alone.

'Where is everyone?'

'I told them to go, and they went. I need to speak to you.'

Oh, no. This is bad news, Cara thought. Whenever the

two of them were alone, something happened. It was a bad, bad idea to be alone with Dan. As a matter of fact, an entourage was the best thing that had ever happened to her. She took a step back, but Dan crossed his arms and looked at her as if she was a child getting caught playing truant.

'Are you going to stop backing away from me long enough to let me apologise to you?'

'Ap…' Her voice was hoarse, despite the relief. 'Apologise?'

'Yeah, apologise. Dan Hunter, apologising. Ring your editor, put it on the front page.'

'What for?'

Dan's eyes softened, making him look like his old self, and the part within her that still remembered the sweet, lovely Dan tugging at her to go to him, like an impatient child tugging on a mother's hand towards the playground. But she held that part of her back, even though – dammit! – she could already imagine the warm feel of his skin under her hands.

'Yesterday. I was way out of line for making comments about your sexuality. They were inappropriate and hurtful.'

'They weren't hurtful.' Cara looked down. She'd been indignant but, in fact, the words *had* stung. For the life of her, she couldn't understand why, but she didn't want Dan to think of her as someone who couldn't be passionately abandoned in bed. Or wouldn't wear a red suspender belt!

'Well, even if they didn't hurt you, it hurt me to say them. You're far from being Royal Command Performance material, and I know it.'

Memories of that night liquefied something hot and bubbling within her, and she had to keep herself from gasping as she looked up to meet Dan's sultry gaze, knowing that he was thinking exactly the same thing. For a few static-crackling moments, he held her gaze, then cleared his throat and shook his head slightly, as if to clear it.

'Anyway, I had no right to discuss your relationship with Robert...'

Mention of Robert brought intense colour to her face, and Cara looked down once again, mortified by the fact that in that gaze she had shared with Dan she had been unfaithful to Robert several times over, and in several inventive positions. She was supposed to be thinking of a way to reconcile with him!

In a split second, Dan was standing in front of her, lifting her chin, looking into her eyes.

'Cara.' His voice was gentle, a caress. 'What's wrong?'

Cara swallowed hard. This was a dangerous man. If his mere voice had her skin yearning for his touch, she had to put some distance between them.

'Nothing's wrong!' she denied with as much nonchalance as she could muster. 'What are you talking about?'

'Oh, don't give me that, Cara. It's me, remember? When there's something wrong, it always shows on your face.'

'It does?' she croaked.

She couldn't help thinking of Robert the night before, or any other time, come to think of it. Robert never suspected – or even asked – if she'd ever had a rough day. Well, she resolved, that was going to change. If she and Robert were going to make a go of it, they would have to be more communicative, more...

Her thoughts trailed off as she felt Dan's fingers, soft as butterflies around her lips, then up her cheeks to her earlobes. She closed her eyes and sighed almost inaudibly as pinpoints of pleasure sparked her skin and rippled in little waves that lapped at parts of her he hadn't even laid a hand on. Dan's touches were like promises. Promises of luxuriant, unimaginable sensuousness. When was the last time she had been touched like this? There hadn't *been* a last time, a little voice inside her pointed out. She had never been touched like this before.

'Your skin is so fair,' Dan murmured. 'When you're upset, you go pink around your lips, and on your earlobes.'

'Mmm…what?' Cara, dimly aware that he had spoken, opened her eyes.

'You're obviously upset. No one's going to benefit from the journalist being upset, are they?'

'I see.'

At the end of the day, it all boiled down to business. Like Robert said, scratching each other's backs. She needed this job, and Dan needed her to promote his stupid movie. She knew the score – so why did it make her feel so empty?

'"I see"? I don't think so. Now you're getting even more pink.'

'No, I'm not!' she said stupidly, looking down.

Dan took hold of her chin once more and raised it up. 'I'm tired of arguing with you,' he said softly, blue eyes clear and earnest. 'You and I, we don't talk very well. Perhaps we should just stop talking altogether. You know, the last time we actually got on, was when we *got on…*'

He brought his mouth to hers and, as he parted her lips, she noticed that he didn't close his eyes, so she took his cue. Open eye kisses were playful, light, and friendly, right? Wrong. The look of his eyes in this intimate moment tapped into some inner drive, and she discovered herself wanting to kiss him back, to give herself. Into his deep blue eyes she dived, into a pool of clean fresh water, while at the same time anchored to Dan in the languorous, slick dance of lips on lips, tongue entwining tongue. Just a kiss, and yet it was the most powerfully erotic experience of her life. She was breathing his breath, coursing in his bloodstream, their bodies asking questions only the other could answer.

As the kiss deepened, Dan's eyes deepened too. They grew dark and stormy as passion gathered force and the motion and moistness of their lips became an echo of their bodies' awakening. Dan's hands fell from her face, to her shoulders, down her spine, to her hips. He put each of his big hands on her pelvis, taking hold of it and pivoting it to fit snugly against his. It felt so right, so more-ish, that she cupped his deliciously tight butt in her hands and brought him even closer, grinding against him, feeling the reality and substance of his arousal, as well as her own. This was hot. Hot and, somehow…special.

He broke the kiss off slowly, nipping and sucking at her lower lip, and smiled down at her, not unlike the cat that's got the cream. 'I knew it.'

The self-satisfied conceit of those three little words were like a bucket of cold water. With ice cubes floating in it. Her heart was still racing, and her lips zinging with the spice of his kiss, and it took an iron will to shift her concentration away from the treachery of her body's reaction. What on earth had she been thinking? He had honed right in on her vulnerability and taken advantage, all to prove the point he had been making since they had met again…that he could have her! Just like he could have anyone and anything. *And I went and nearly proved him right* she thought with fresh horror. The way she'd responded! Like she'd never been kissed before. Like she wasn't worried to death over Robert. Like she believed all the claptrap about being the object of his undying love since the day they were born. Like she believed he wanted her, the person. Like…like she wanted him *back*, for heaven's sakes!

She straightened her spine and took three steps back,

out of his grasp. 'You knew what? That I'm a wild one? Sorry Dan, I've heard that one before. Aren't comedians supposed to be on the lookout for original material?'

Dan could only expel his breath and shake his head. 'I don't believe it,' he finally said. 'You actually managed to talk yourself out of it.'

'Out of what?' Cara replied primly, straightening her jacket.

'You know what! You and I both felt it!'

Cara swallowed hard and, with all her might and mind, concentrated on summoning up a careless smile. 'What? Horny? I thought we'd established I wasn't the Royal Command Performance type.'

He narrowed his eyes and with long strides crossed the distance between them. 'Oh, I know you're not the passionless type. And I also know that wasn't just horny. It was…'

'Nice.' Cara crossed her arms in front of her, erecting a barrier between them. 'Thanks, Dan. I needed that.'

'What?' His voice was incredulous.

'Your experience with women has made you very perceptive. Robert and I had a…misunderstanding. I suppose I needed comforting, I needed…kissing, and you picked right up on it. It did me good. Thank you.'

'Well,' Dan said with his hands on hips, voice dripping sarcasm, 'As an international sex symbol, you can imagine I'm glad to be of assistance. Is there anything else I could do for you? Let's see…the *full* service, perhaps?'

He roughly reached out for her before she could step back any further and pulled her to him, sneaking his fingers just under the hem of her skirt, and gently stroking the delicate skin of the back of her thighs. Her leg muscles turned to rags, barely supporting her as they yielded to more important matters – sensation, desire. But even if she had had enough muscle tone to fight him, his strong upper arms held her captive.

'Oh, I know I'm not a real man, like the real men you prefer,' he urgently whispered in her ear, his breathe sending tremors through her. 'I'm not intellectual, or mature, or worthy of your respect, but you don't need that, right? Who needs to feel like they fit together up here,' – he tapped both their heads – 'when they fit together so well down here…?'

Dan pulled her even closer and in semblance of what had just happened, ground her hips against his. But this felt nothing like before! Inexplicable tears sprang to Cara's eyes.

'Dan! Dan, please don't…!'

'Why not? You just said nothing significant happened between us! You were horny, and you took advantage of it to help you feel better, and now I'm offering to go the distance for you. What more can you ask for? I can do horny. I can do horny so well…'

She gasped as Dan began to kiss a burning band around her throat, his hands on her thighs trailing upwards to a place that was betraying her by pulsating with heat and need under his touch. *Yeah*, some part of her thought, *he can do horny really well. And so can I.* But this felt totally, absolutely, unequivocally, *wrong*.

'Stop it!' she exclaimed, finally finding her breath and enough strength to push him away.

'Well, well, well.' His voice, as he looked into her glittering eyes, was as breathless as hers. 'I guess horny is not what you want, after all.'

Cara held the mobile phone to her ear, even though she knew having it switched on inside the hospital was against the rules. It was only for a moment and, besides, this was an emergency.

Standing away from the crowd squeezing into the cancer ward, she waved a silent hello to the photographer from the *Clarion*. HTICH's donation of the 'Jolly Trolley' – that was its name, newly painted in sunny yellow letters – was going great guns. Dan, accompanied by other Tiches, had already addressed the assembled media, and they were now moving through the ward, interacting with the children and smiling for the cameras.

She had already observed enough and taken ample notes. Now she was dialling Robert's number again, with fresh desperation, as if she were in some kind of danger and only Robert could rescue her.

'This is Robert Neville. Please leave a message.'

'Robert, if you're there, please pick up.' She took a deep breath, and felt the hot sting of tears as her plea wasn't heeded. *Beep.* 'Robert, please…I'm working tonight so I can't see you, but I really need to speak to you. I'm so sorry about last night. I acted like a stupid kid…'

'Who says kids are stupid?'

Cara started as she saw Marie, in a wheelchair beside her, being pushed by a young nurse. Cara quickly prayed for some sort of composure and, switching off her mobile, smiled and crouched down beside her. She felt her heart contract when she saw how pale and weak she looked. Poor kid.

'Hi, Marie. Sorry. If I ever thought kids are stupid, you're quickly changing my mind.'

Marie peered at her. 'Are you OK?'

Cara nodded, probably too vigorously, she belatedly thought. 'I'm…I'm fine.'

'Sure?'

'Yeah, I'm sure. How are you today?'

Marie shrugged. 'Not so good. I've just had some tests

done. Doctor Phoebe wants to speak to my Mum, so I reckon it's bad news.'

'Oh, come on, Marie.' Cara forced a smile. 'You don't know that…'

'Oh yes, I do.' Marie smiled for real. 'Just like this fake smile you're wearing right now. Grown-ups have a whole heap of facial expressions that are supposed to hide what's going on from us kids.'

Cara laughed.

'Marie, your room is full of photographers and reporters and things,' the nurse said, leaning forward. 'Would you like to wait with me in the nurses' station for a little while?'

'Oh, that's OK, Jamie. Cara will take me out to the patio for a little while. Won't you, Cara?'

'Sure.'

Cara followed Marie's directions and pushed the wheelchair to a paved courtyard that was like a different world. There were palm trees, clusters of honey-sweet grevillea with chattering lorikeets feeding among them, and raised flowerbeds tumbling flowers like treasure chests overflowing with jewels. There were also tables, park benches, and a playground protected from the brutal Queensland sun by a winged, sail-like canopy.

Cara parked Marie's wheelchair under a banana palm, and sat down on a park bench. Marie breathed in tremulously and smiled. The two shared the same colouring, but Marie's looked paler than Cara's. It gave her skin a fragile translucence, like that of fine bone china.

'Have you spoken to your Dad about me yet?'

'Not yet. I'll see him tomorrow and I'll tell him then. OK?'

'OK.'

The two sat in silence, but it was a companionable

silence, as they soaked in the warmth and fragrance of the air around them. Cara took a deep breath…

'So, who's Robert?'

… and choked on it as Marie blurted out the indelicate question with a cherubic smile.

'Wh-what? How much of what I said on the phone did you hear?'

'Oh – all of it. So? Who is he?'

'Umm, Robert Neville,' she said with forced casualness. 'He's a journalist. Heard of him?'

'That's not what I meant and you know it, Cara. I meant, who is he *to you*?'

Cara shifted in her seat uncomfortably. *Marie*, Cara thought, *would make a fine journalist herself. Preferably the abrasive, microphone-pushed-in-the-mouth, foot-in-the-door, the-whole-truth-exposed, television journalist.*

She screwed up her face, in a constipated effort to get the answer out right. 'Well, let's see. Robert was…I mean, Robert is my…er, that is to say, we are…'

What the heck were they? It wasn't dating, and it certainly wasn't 'going out'. He wasn't a boyfriend because she was too old to have one and he was too old to be one, and he wasn't a partner because they only shared a certain part of their lives together. So… What did you call it? It was free, it was easy, it was convenient. A mutually advantageous arrangement. But, she thought, looking at Marie's sweet face, how did she say that without sounding cold and mercenary? Or – more likely, now that she knew the child a little better – without Marie bursting into gales of laughter?

'…friends. We are friends.'

'A man friend?'

'Uh-huh.'

Marie looked up to the sky, a thoughtful look on her freckled face. 'Hmm. My Mum used to have a man friend. Then she got rid of him. Said he wasn't a friend *or* a man.'

Cara choked a second time, but in shocked laughter this time. Shock at what Marie had said, and that she'd found it so funny.

'Well,' Cara finally said when she calmed down, 'Robert's both.'

'Then why did he make you cry?'

Looking into Marie's eyes, Cara saw she was a smart, smart cookie indeed. She had an angelic face that lulled you into thinking she was asking totally innocent questions, but she knew exactly what she was saying, and what point she was getting at, just like she had the first time they'd met.

'Hey…how old are you, anyway?'

'I'll be fourteen in a few weeks. Thought I was younger, didn't you?' Marie's smile was cheeky, as if this sort of thing happened all the time. 'It's all the cancer treatment and, besides, I'm small for my age. Anyway, stop trying to change the subject and answer the question!'

No, she realised, it didn't do to underestimate Marie, nor to insult her intelligence by skirting the questions.

'Well…let's just say he didn't appreciate it when I didn't "straighten" my writing.' *Or my mind.* She thought it, but didn't say it.

'Then how good a friend could he be? When I first got sick, my Mum told me I would find out who my real friends were. Some of them stopped seeing me. They didn't like thinking of me as someone different to who they thought I was.' She shrugged. 'Big deal. In the end, you're better off with someone who accepts you the way you are, good or bad.'

'Well, this is a little different, Marie. Some relationships have problems that have to be sorted out. Robert and I just need to talk about things, that's all.'

'You know,' Marie said, nodding in the direction of her ward, 'I bet he wouldn't mind how un-straight you were.'

'"He" who?' she asked, with a sense of impending doom.

'You know. *Him*.' Marie emphasised. 'Doody the Clown. Dan Hunter.'

Cara shook her head. 'Uh-uh. No-ooooo. Da…Mr Hunter and I have a professional relationship, and only for a little while, while I write an article about him.'

'No you don't.'

'Yes we…hey! Didn't your Mum ever teach you not to argue with a grown-up?' Cara laughed.

'Actually,' Marie smiled back smugly, 'my mum told me to *always* argue, *always* question. It's being sick, you see. She says that no one can tell me what's going to happen to me. Only I can decide that.'

'Well,' Cara put a finger on Marie's nose, 'both you and your Mum are very clever. So, I can say that no one can tell me what's going to happen to me, either.'

'But you'd be perfect for each other!'

'How did you work that out? He and I are completely different, we're from two totally different worlds!'

Marie sighed impatiently. 'So? There's more chemistry between you guys than… than…Bonnie and Clyde!'

'Marie, this is real life, not the movies,' she said softly.

Talking to Marie had been like participating in some sort of hyperactive sport, ducking and weaving, pushing and pulling, skirting and skimming, catching and throwing, running and dancing, all with words. She smiled to herself. She had thoroughly enjoyed it.

Marie, like many children, had made her an instant, intimate friend. She was totally open, and Cara had followed her lead. And for all her illness, she had made Cara laugh and laugh. *I'd love to see her again*, Cara thought, and was taken aback. Robert insisted that the appeal of having children was in raising carbon copies of yourself – 'the ultimate act of narcissism'. But Cara couldn't imagine Marie being a carbon copy of anyone, and had enjoyed her company *as a person*. Ah well, even if she and Robert didn't have children, there was no reason why she couldn't have a relationship with this child.

She stopped at the nurses' station on the way out. 'Jamie?' she asked the young nurse who had been wheeling Marie earlier. 'Is it OK if I pop in to see Marie on Sunday? I thought I'd bring some autographed books from my dad and stay for a chat.'

Jamie sighed and shrugged. 'What can I tell you? I really don't know. I'm not sure about the details but things aren't looking good.'

Cara felt a fearful rush of adrenaline through her body, setting her heart racing. 'But – but it's only two days!'

'This isn't an ingrown toenail we're talking about, Ms St John, it's cancer. Even in the best case scenario, the only thing anyone can do is take it one day at a time.'

Cara slumped, her eyes fixed on some invisible object at her feet. That any child should have to die had always been inexplicable. But knowing Marie, the thought of it happening to her was more than that. It hurt. She wiped her damp palms on her skirt and looked up. She was afraid of asking, but knew she had to.

'You mean – Marie could actually…die?'

Jamie gave her a compassionate smile. 'No one can say that, least of all me. What I can tell you is that it won't happen if Marie has anything to say about it. Still, the poor kid has been fighting this since she was eight years old and she's plain old exhausted. If you want to see her again, don't leave it too long, OK?'

'OK.' Cara pinched the bridge of her nose and closed her eyes.

Jamie moved from behind the counter and put a hand on Cara's arm. 'Listen, Ms St John – Cara – I don't mean to be disrespectful, but your attitude isn't going to help Marie. As a matter of fact, you know she'd hate it. The best thing you can do is put it out of your mind for now. Have a wonderful weekend so you can tell Marie all about it on Sunday, OK?'

Cara looked up and smiled gratefully. 'Thanks. You must think I'm some sort of drama queen. Here I am, almost a stranger, and all of you here who know and love these children…well, let's just say you have my utmost respect.'

'It's a privilege being here for them. What they give to us far outweighs any of the pain, believe me.'

Cara decided to take the stairs. In the stairwell, she took a few minutes to take some steadying breaths and clear her mind. Jamie was right. She wasn't being callous in deciding not to worry about what might happen to Marie; it was a matter of being able to function, and honouring Marie's wonderful attitude. There were other, more immediate things to worry about right now.

Like Robert! Cara thought as she climbed back into the van. *And Dan*, she added when she saw him waiting inside. *All I have to do is just survive Dan until I can get in touch with Robert.* Once she talked with Robert, got things out in the open, and re-established a new sense of harmony, things would be back to normal – at least some of the way. It would do until Dan was out of her life in twelve hours and three days. She smiled inwardly at her calculation. Hadn't Jamie told her to take things one day at a time?

'Are you OK?' Dan asked.

Dan had a disturbing habit of sussing out when she had things on her mind, and considering what had happened the last time he had thought she needed comforting, this was bad news. Even though the memory of his kiss sent warm pulses through her, she knew she had to stay cool and in control – and never closer than arm's length. It was survival. Her own, and that of her relationship with Robert.

'Yes. Why wouldn't I be?'

'Oh, no reason.' He paused, then came in for the kill. 'Unless, of course, you want to pounce on me again like you did earlier.'

'POUNCE?' Anna turned around, so Cara lowered her voice to a harsh whisper. '*I* do not "pounce", as you put it.'

'Well, you pounced on me.'

'I *what*? It was you! *You* took my face in your hands. *You*…touched me. *You* kissed me.'

'It was a mental pounce. You wanted me to kiss you, so I did.'

'Oh – oh, that's a good one, Mr Cro-Magnon! What are you going to tell me now – that when a woman says "no", she actually means, "yes"? Perhaps you'd like to demonstrate? I'll untie my hair and let you drag me around by it, if you like.'

'Off you go on your little hobby horse, Cara,' Dan chuckled. 'If it helps you ignore that you liked it – no, correction, that you *loved* it – then giddy up! We both know what happened.'

Cara bit her lip. Damn him! Maybe she should just get used to this corner he kept backing her into. Get a comfy chair. A nice picture to look at. A vase of flowers. Obviously she couldn't pretend she hadn't enjoyed it, but admitting she had would just be another stroke on his proud, purring ego. What was left?

Silence!

She had tried everything from common sense to childish arguing, but not this. Wasn't the classic strategy for dealing with a tease at school, 'Ignore him and he'll just go away'?

Cara stared straight ahead.

'Cara?'

Dan leaned forward and put his face right in hers, but Cara's gaze didn't waver from that invisible point in some more peaceful distance.

'Cara? Cara! Oh, I see. You're giving me the silent treatment, right? OK. Cara, if you don't talk to me, I'll yell.'

Cara stared straight ahead.

'I mean it. I really will yell.'

Cara said nothing, eyes barely blinking.

'I'll yell really, really loud.'

Cara was silent.

'CAAAAAAAAAAAAAAARAAAAAAAAAAAA!! !!!'

Cara jumped, and Anna screamed. Cory slammed on the brakes, flung open the van door, and yelled out a guttural 'haaaaa!', brandishing karate-chop hands.

'Mr Hunter, are you OK?' he asked, wildly looking around the van for kidnappers, or terrorists, or tabloid journalists.

'Fine. It's Cara. She didn't want to talk to me, but I think she will now.'

Cara pointed at him. 'Of all the stupid, childish…'

She couldn't continue. She was laughing.

chapter seven

'Dan! Darling!'

Cara heard the familiar voice of Denise, Dan's mother, and then the booming tones of Dr Wayne Hunter, his father, as they entered the hotel lobby. They descended on their son with kisses and shoulder-clapping hugs.

'Hi, Mum. What's up, Doc?' Dan said as he came up for air.

'What's up Doc yourself,' his father replied. 'This is one hell of a place!'

Dan's parents always talked simultaneously, either finishing each other's sentences, or each going off on different tangents that one was always expected to follow.

'The others have all gone up to their rooms...'

'To raid the minibar and steal the towels, I bet. That's what you get for offering to put us up here, son. Those siblings of yours are going to make sure they get your money's worth...'

'...so your Dad and I thought we'd wait here for you. What a lovely hotel...'

'...and I must say I've taken advantage myself. All I've got to do is mention the Hunter name and free drinks magically appear at my fingertips...'

And suddenly...

'Cara, you lovely girl, how are you?'

She couldn't escape the hugs and kisses either. The Hunters always kissed each other 'hello' and 'goodbye', no matter where they were going or where they'd been, and since Cara always joined in the throng, she was always a part of all the touchy-feely stuff. Not that her parents were stand-offish but, by the time you'd hugged and kissed your way through the eleven Hunters, you felt like you'd been put through a very loving wringing-machine.

Wayne hugged her and whispered in her ear, 'No wonder Dan didn't tell us you were the journalist with him. He wanted to keep you all to himself!'

Cara blushed. 'Really, Wayne, it's business. He *did* tell you it's business, didn't he?' Oh, please let him have told them it was business! Both sets of parents had been trying to match-make them all their lives, and she didn't need the extra pressure right now.

'Yeah, he did,' Wayne winked. 'But nothing's stopping you two from mixing business with pleasure, right?'

'Oh, Wayne, please!' Denise playfully shoved Wayne aside. 'Leave the poor girl alone. Can't you see she's embarrassed? Anyway,' she grasped Cara's shoulders and looked her up and down, 'you look beautiful, as usual, but I see what your mum means when she says you look peaky!'

Cara cast a pregnant glance at Dan. 'It's stress.'

'Stress? Oh dear, never mind. We'll have such fun tonight! It'll be just like when you were little, you and the Hunters, all taking up an entire row at the cinema…'

'What do you mean?' Cara looked from Denise, to Wayne, and finally to Dan.

'The première, dear.'

'What? Oh, no,' she laughed, holding her palms in front of her. 'I'm going strictly as a spectator, representing the *Clarion*. I really can't be a part of it with all of you…'

'What nonsense! Who says you can't?' Denise looked back at the two men. 'She can, can't she, Wayne?'

'Of course she can. She must.'

'But...' Her voice against Denise's was as futile as a fan in a hurricane.

'She can, can't she, Dan?'

'Of course she can. She *must*.'

Dan smiled straight at her, eyes crinkling at the corners wickedly. *He's loving it!* she thought. *He knows I can withstand him, but not the Hunter mob en masse.*

'But my dear, there's no way you can go tonight in that little suit. Noooo. We'll need to get you something suitable; pun unintentional.' Denise placed an arm around her shoulders and began leading her to the lifts. 'We'll go upstairs and get Danielle, Daria and Wendy. They'd love to go shopping with us for something glamorous. Dalton's here too. He'll just have to do something with your hair...'

Cara looked back, a pleading look on her face. Dan wiggled his fingers and mouthed out 'toodle-oo'.

Oh, Dan Hunter, you'll keep!

Daria Hunter stood behind Cara, hands on her eyes.

'You're peeking!'

'I'm not!' Cara protested.

'All right. I'll move my hands now, but don't open your eyes until I tell you to, OK?'

'Fine, Daria. Now will you just get on with it? I have work to do, you know.'

'I don't think Dan will be letting you do much work tonight. Take a look.'

Daria removed her hands and Cara, sighing impatiently, opened her eyes.

'Oh. My. Gosh.'

'Well?' Daria and Dalton smiled expectantly.

Denise, Dan's sisters Wendy, Danielle, Daria, and his brother Dalton had pushed and pulled Cara through a tortuous shopping expedition that had pitted her conservative tastes against theirs. She didn't stand a chance. Denise wanted her to make Dan's eyes pop out. Wendy was extremely pregnant and wanted the vicarious pleasure of buying a little slinky something a third of her current size. Danielle was an arts student with gothic tastes who laughed at everything Cara picked. Daria was a party girl, and wanted her to dress like an 18-year-old disco queen. And flamboyant Dalton wanted her to dress in something with 'vavoom'. In the end, Cara had gone back to the hotel with Denise and Wendy to work in peace on her laptop, and left Danielle, Daria and Dalton to make the final decision. Big mistake.

'The underwear is nice,' she said. 'Now – where's the actual dress?'

'Cara!'

It was a chorus of dismay, but Dalton took charge. 'Look at yourself.'

'I am!'

'No.' He grabbed her chin and forced her to look in the mirror once more. 'I mean *really* look at yourself.'

She was wearing a sky blue slip. Well, all right, not just any slip – a long, very expensive slip, from a chi-chi new designer, but a slip nonetheless. The heaviness of the fine shot silk jersey draped and clung to her every curve and, as she turned, the opalised seed beads embroidered on to it in a curlicue that wound around from her breasts to her waist and the small of her bare back, caught the light and winked suggestively. Very high, strappy gold sandals – a total nightmare to walk in. And the slit. The very, very high slit up her left leg that, along with the clinging of the fabric, ensured she would either have to wear a G-string, or go without panties altogether. The G-string had won.

Dalton had done her hair. As Cara feared, he had

wanted to bring out the curls. He loved her curls. Raved about the curls. Told her how much women paid for such curls. He had gone on and on and on until Cara had yelled, 'All right! Have the stupid curls!' Dalton had grinned, rubbed his palms together, and set to work. Now, she had to admit, the mane around her head and shoulders looked quite spectacular. Her hair first thing in the morning did, in fact, sport what Dan had long ago called the 'finger in the electric socket' look, but Dalton had tamed the frizz and pop with jars of pomades and unguents and other mysterious things. He had transformed her explosive curls to a tumble of round, glossy, voluptuous locks that shone like a halo around her already shimmering figure.

Cara sighed. 'Oh, I'll pass, I suppose…'

'Cara!'

Another dismayed chorus, but Cara shrugged. 'Guys, I know you've gone to a lot of trouble, but this really isn't *me*…'

'And how would you know what is "you" until you've given every possible "you" a chance?' Danielle was philosophical.

'She's right,' Dalton said. 'You've got to try it. At least, just this once. I mean, not even the Queen dresses like the Queen all the time, if you know what I'm saying.'

Daria put her hand on her hips. 'What are you guys *talking* about? Who cares whether or not this is her, or could be her, or whatever? She looks hot! That's all that matters.'

'Oh, all right!' Cara threw her hands up in the air. 'Have it your own way. You three have got your own way for far too long, if you ask me.'

Dalton, Danielle and Daria smiled back cheekily, looking the picture of their fame as 'The Triple Terror'.

They were the youngest of the Hunter clan, and their arrival in the world could only have been planned by a deity with a wicked sense of humour. After bearing six children, Denise hadn't planned on another pregnancy, but cheerfully welcomed the news. The welcome had turned to disbelief a couple of months later, however, when an ultrasound revealed she was expecting triplets. Six, nine, what's the difference, easygoing Denise and Wayne had shrugged when they'd got used to the idea. But the triplets had indeed been different. They were so darned adorable that they were not only spoilt by their six older siblings, but indulged by everyone in Toongalla, creating the monster that was 'The Triple Terror'.

Cara sat down to work a little longer while the others got ready. She picked up her mobile phone and swore. A missed call, from Robert no less! She tried ringing him back but he had already left the *Clarion*. She was working tonight, so when would she be able to catch up with him?

A sudden thought made her break out in a cold sweat.

Oh, no.

Work.

She had told Robert she was working tonight, and she would be…except that she'd be on the late news and tomorrow's paper, a glamour puss tripping down the red carpet with Dan and the rest of the Hunter clan!

What would Robert say? It would the last straw, of course. What had she been thinking, allowing herself to be swayed like this? Particularly after all but accusing Robert of selling out because of Heather! What a hypocrite. Instead of covering the event objectively from the sidelines like she was supposed to if she was half the journalist she said she was, there she would be, part of all the glitz!

Cara put a hand on her hot forehead. She had to

think of something. There had to be a way out. That's it – rationally, calmly, she could explain it to them. Tell Dan that she would still cover the première, as arranged, but from the sidelines. Appeal to Denise and Wayne, and help them understand that she had her professional integrity. Thank Danielle, Daria and Dalton for all their trouble. Tell the rest of the Hunters – Damian, Willow, Dimity, Warren, and Wendy, and their assorted spouses and kids – that she'd catch up with them at the barbecue tomorrow, and that she'd bring chocolate ripple cake.

Talk to all of them. One small, insignificant Cara St John. Against eleven rowdy Hunters!

There was nothing for it.

She had to run away.

She would go home, get changed, go to the theatre, and join the assembled media. Swishing down a red carpet hadn't been a part of the *Clarion*'s deal with Dan, after all, so her job was safe. There was nothing to fear.

So why was she shutting down her laptop with as much care as if she were deactivating a bomb? Why was she tiptoeing out, oh-so-careful not to disturb Danielle and Daria in the bathroom? Why was she opening the door like a jewel thief cracking a safe, making sure it didn't creak?

There was no time to ponder the answer to any of these questions. She took a deep breath and walked out.

Straight into Dan's chest.

She knew it was Dan's chest without looking up. In the farce that her life had become, it would have to be, wouldn't it? Besides, with her entire face in his pristine white shirt, she smelt him, or rather the delicious undertone of the ocean, coming through the refined aroma of his cologne. So much for arm's length!

The heat emanating through his shirt added to her own

and she blushed as she heard his voice, hushed and somehow reverent, speak her name.

'Cara.'

She looked up, and was amazed at the combined desire and tenderness in his eyes as he skimmed her glittering body with his eyes. Cara's skin reacted as if he were caressing her, and her heart spilled over as if welcoming a long-lost lover. Although she realised that the way she looked had turned him on, suddenly, what she was wearing seemed irrelevant. With a split second's insight, she knew that she had seen Dan's gaze only because she had, for once, let her guard down. With her guard down, she would feel such delicious glances like small flames licking at her body even if she were wearing sackcloth.

But this was crazy! Only a moment ago she had been worried sick over what Robert might think! *Maybe*, she thought, *it's time to wake up, grow up, and admit Dan is attractive*. Wasn't that why he was desired by all the straight women and a good portion of the non-straight men, in the civilised world? Admit the attraction, and deal with it. But remember the facts. He was not the man for her and, right now, she had to ensure that the man who *was* didn't see her cavorting with a movie star.

She put her hands on his chest to push herself away, but of their own accord, her fingers spread and strained to feel the warm firm smoothness of his golden skin through the fabric. His muscles weren't chiselled out of rock like a bodybuilder's, but each one was distinct under her sensitive fingertips, like a map in relief. Her breathing deepened as she realised she wanted to keep feeling, keep running her hands over not just his chest but the rest of him. She wanted to divest him of every scrap of this ridiculous monkey suit. It might have been Armani, but it wasn't Dan Hunter. Dan belonged in nothing, nothing at all. The only thing that should be draped on his gorgeous body was her own.

'Cara, you are superb.'

She looked up again, almost afraid of being consumed by his eyes, or maybe consuming him with her own. His hair was brushed back, showing his beautiful face in a new, intense light. *But* – she struggled to remember what it was that she was supposed to remember – *keep in mind this is physical, this is normal. You're no different to any one of the other million women who drool over his close-up in the glossy magazines.*

'Umm, yeah, you too. You look…' Admit the attraction, deal with it, and get it out of the way, common sense spoke. Cara obeyed. 'Very handsome. I can see why you were voted "Sexiest Man Alive".'

Changing the focus to his public persona seemed to do the trick. He smiled sadly, as if aware that an important moment had been lost, and took a step backwards.

'Thanks. I aim to please.'

The flat tone of his voice pierced Cara as his silence had that time in the van. But, surely, this was totally different! It wasn't malice – she just couldn't afford to lose sight of the big picture here. Risk her long-term relationship with Robert over a transient attraction? No. If putting first things first hurt sometimes, then so be it.

Dan nodded at the laptop slung over her shoulder. 'Going somewhere?'

'Yeah…' Cara bit her lip. 'Listen, Dan, I really can't walk down that red carpet with you.'

'Oh, I know that.'

Cara furrowed her brow. 'You do?'

'Of course. I'm being accompanied by my two leading ladies.'

'Wh-what?'

'Jenna Stephens, and Ebony Jaxxon. They arrived

from Los Angeles just a few hours ago. Heard of them?'

Cara nodded grimly. Jenna Stephens was a two-block-buster veteran. And Ebony Jaxxon – weird name spelling courtesy of her numerologist – was a model-turned-actor, on her first foray into acting. Both of them were gorgeous.

'Anyway,' Dan added as he turned to go, 'I just came to tell you three that we're all having drinks in my suite before we go. Everyone wants to meet Jenna and Ebony. Tell Daria and Danielle, would you please?'

It was Cara's turn to feel deflated.

Everyone wanted to meet Jenna and Ebony, except her. She felt lacklustre beside these two goddesses with hair up to here, blindingly white teeth from here to there, hipbones sticking out to there, and décolletage down to heaven-knew-where. She sat in a corner making mental notes, sullen as she observed them hold court, with no one quite so attentive as Dan. *The court jester*, she thought wryly, turning to look out of the window.

'Champagne?'

Dan's smooth voice made her whip around. He prof-fered a crystal flute, and his playful smile and the rakish air that his now-crooked bow tie lent him did nothing to dispel her mood.

'Thanks, but no thanks. I…don't drink.' *At least, not any more*, she silently vowed.

'Not even to help me celebrate?'

'Especially not to help you celebrate.'

Dan feigned a hurt look. 'Ouch! What did I do to deserve that?'

Cara sighed. 'Look, Dan, I'm sorry, but you know being here in this capacity wasn't my idea. It was your folks', and you encouraged it. This isn't my place.'

'But this is part of my week, isn't it? And aren't you

supposed to be writing about "A Week in the Life of Dan Hunter"?'

'Yes, *this* is a part of your week, but…' She put a hand on her chest for emphasis. '*I'm* not.'

He cast a direct gaze at her. 'Oh yes you are. And more.'

He walked away to mingle among his guests, and Cara was left speechless once more in his wake.

As everyone started filing out to the limousines that were waiting outside to drive them to the theatre, Cara suddenly thought that being a member of the hallowed party wasn't that big a deal if Dan was going to have two Hollywood divas on his muscular arms. She climbed into one of the limousines with Warren and Damian, Damian's wife Louise, and their four kids, who were behaving like cardboard cut-outs of normal children.

'My goodness, Louise.' Damian nodded towards the children with his usual deadpan humour. 'They're actually subdued. How long do you think it'll last?'

'Just start pushing buttons, darling, that'll keep them quiet.'

Damian demonstrated the minibar, the power windows, the sunroof, and the television, and they all laughed at the children's progressively wider eyes and mouths.

Suddenly Sophie, the oldest child, pointed out of the tinted windows. 'Look!'

It was worth pointing at. Someone had gone to a lot of trouble to make sure that this looked like a typically excessive eighties do, and the outside of the theatre had not only been embellished with a red carpet, but also a huge, top lit 'Mikhail McHale, Double Agent' billboard, bleachers for the fans, searchlights, and a gold canopy for guests to walk under. A roar from the crowd rose up like a wave as the limousines rounded the corner into the street.

Dan's car was last, and Cara was dismayed to realise that they were to be the first sacrificial lambs. As the chauffeur opened the door of their limousine, the cries and screeches rose and rose until she thought her eardrums would burst. But as they stepped out on to the carpet and the fans saw that it was neither Dan nor his leading ladies, it died down. Damian's children waved shyly at the crowd, as they had no doubt been coached to do, and smiled at the lights popping all around them.

Cara was frozen like a rabbit in a car's headlights. It wasn't until Warren put his arm around her waist and said, 'Come on, champ, let's get this show on the road,' that she was able to move her feet, after giving him a grateful smile. Flashes were going off so fast that she felt like she was in a disco under strobe lights, and the unreal attention focused on them gave her a feeling of disembodiment, as if this was her body walking and smiling, but she was really somewhere else.

Body and person, however, came together again quite violently at the sound: 'Hey, Cara! Is yours a cushy job or what?'

Cara squinted against the glare. *Of course, what else?* she thought as she saw the distinctive logo on the microphone and cameras. A crew from the Channel 11 news. Heather's news.

'Cara, how about a nice smile for Robert?' This from a photographer from the *Antipodean*.

Cara closed her eyes briefly. *Give me strength*, she prayed, and took a deep breath. She placed her own arm around Warren's waist and gave him and the cameras what she hoped was a disarming, happy smile. She was aware that the people out there were her peers, and that she could now be the loser in that bloodiest of sports – media turning against one of their own. The thought made her break out in a cold sweat, and she thankfully entered the theatre lobby and took cover behind a marble pillar. Here she was safe and free to watch the spectacle outside.

The crescendo outside reached peak hysteria as Dan unfolded himself out of his limousine, and helped Jenna Stephens and Ebony Jaxxon out. Inside, all was calm and relatively sane. Outside, it was a different world. As Dan and the two women made it slowly down the strip, Cara was never more keenly aware of how different his life was from hers. She watched him flash his killer smile, wave, and reach out to shake hands and accept feverish teenage kisses. The women took the carpet like a catwalk, posing, turning, making sure they were caught in every possible angle, bestowing smiles at photographers both close by and further away. Then Dan placed himself between them, and with his strong arms around each of their diminutive waists, murmured private jokes into their shell-like ears. The women threw their heads back in calculated fits of elegant laughter that sent the flashes into a fresh frenzy.

Adulation, that's what it was. They worshipped Dan, Jenna Stephens and Ebony Jaxxon, and yet they were human. It was all an illusion, nothing to do with reality.

And that's the difference between you and I, Dan Hunter, she thought. *You make your living transporting people to another world, and I make mine by bringing them back down to earth again.*

chapter eight

'No way, Cory,' Dan, tossing weekend clothing into a case, was firm. 'I'm not turning up in Toongalla with a bodyguard. It's my hometown! I'll never live it down.'

'But Dan…'

'I said no. Do you want to know what they'll call me if you come along to mind my back? Then have a look through the 'W' section of Anna's Dinkum Dictionary. Stay in Brizzie, do some surfing, see the sights, and meet some women. I'll be safe. When it comes to protecting one of her own, my Mum beats a minder hands down.'

One by one, Dan had got rid of his entourage, except for Scott, of course. And Anna Di Vito, but only by default. He'd tried to reason with her, order her, even bribe her but, no, she was coming. She had the backing of the entire studio, and short of tying her up and shoving her into one of the laundry trolleys, there was nothing he could do to get rid of her. *Really*, he thought, *she should have a German rather than an Italian surname. A name like, say, Doberman, or Rottweiler.*

'It's bad enough that you're taking an entire day off from your promotional duties, without wanting to get rid of the promotional crew as well!' she had said. 'What if the studio was to hear about this?'

What indeed. The studio had a very diplomatic way of getting you to do your duty, and the worst he'd probably get was a slap on the wrist – followed by an expensive gift. He was sure Anna only said this sort of thing to put the wind up people.

Dan was nervous. A lot was riding on getting Cara

away from Brisbane and back to Toongalla. Like Scott said, it was important to get her away from her usual environment, but the fact that she was hurting over another man had added a sense of urgency to the whole operation. A few phone calls and he had found out his name was Robert Neville, journo extraordinaire – even meriting a photograph with his by-line – with the *Antipodean*. It felt like he was running against time, trying to get to her before Robert did but, in truth, he probably already had. You didn't hurt over someone you didn't love, right?

He bit his lip as he viciously shoved socks and underwear into a side pocket of the case. *Think positive!* he admonished himself. One didn't get as far as he had without some sort of positive thinking philosophy, but man, sometimes it was hard. It was hard to hold on when all the evidence pointed in the opposite direction to where he wanted to go. According to the evidence, Cara didn't respect him, and was in love with another man. Jeez! There was a fine, fine line between positive thinking and self-delusion. Which side of the line was he actually on?

For my sake, I hope it's the right one, he thought. He hadn't just rekindled the flame in his heart, but fanned it and poured accelerant on it, until it was raging bush fire, and the thought of not having Cara now was devastating. He had always loved her and known that they were meant for each other, but it hadn't been until now, with a bit of age, maturity, and perspective, that he realised what was at stake if he didn't win her. Even though the thought of waking up in the morning without Cara in his life was terrifying, it would be more than a broken heart. It would mean that the entire life path he had taken had been the wrong one.

Although he regretted not having seen Cara all these

years, he had to admit that maybe, just maybe, she would have been wasted on a younger Dan. Would the younger Dan have realised that beyond his ideals of romance, she completed him? Would he have felt the oneness in their kiss? Would he have felt, when he had seen her dressed up for the première, that his eyes only existed to feast on her beauty?

The image of her last night, like some Titian goddess, had been burned into his mind where it hovered behind his every thought, filling him with an aching need that was the fuel that kept him moving. She had looked so unbelievably beautiful, that it was all he could do not to gather her to him like a precious jewel and take her to some desert island far, far away. But that was impossible, so he had thought that maybe he could play Prince Charming to her Cinderella at the party afterwards. After the screening, however, Dan had been completely surrounded by the usual happy mob of well-wishers, celebrities, socialites, politicians, pundits, fans, and assorted other hangers-on who would dress up and attend the opening of an envelope. Cara wouldn't have been able to get close to him even if she'd wanted to. He had seen her in the distance and caught her eye, and made Tarzan signals indicating the post-screening party, but she'd pointed at her watch and pretended to yawn, and there was nothing he could do but watch her leave. There he'd been, the smash hit movie star, in a sea of people who seemed to like him a lot, feeling cheated and dismayed, wishing he could follow in her wake.

Well, he concluded, hoisting his bag up effortlessly, he was going to make sure that she didn't get away again.

'Right. Anna, Scott, let's go.'

'But, Mr Hunter, what about Ms St John…?'

'We'll pick her up on the way.'

'I don't think she's expecting us.'

'So much the better.'

Getting Cara to Toongalla was all about getting her at a disadvantage. Turning up, unannounced, before she had a chance to prepare herself physically and mentally, was about getting her at a disadvantage too. Although, he had to admit, he was making it up as he went along and didn't quite know what he'd do once he got her at a disadvantage. But one thing was certain – he would do whatever it took.

The Paradise Heights building looked pretty much the sort of place where he had expected her to be – a sea view, a pool, ample security – but quite nice. The apartments had balconies, and he counted up to the eighth one, wondering which of the two balconies was hers. The one with the clotheshorse flapping socks, jocks, and stockings? Or the one with the wrought iron chairs and table, and the miniature orange tree? For his sake, it had better be the orange tree. Jocks meant men, one man in particular. What would he do if he knocked at the door and this Robert person answered? Try to have a sensible, grown-up conversation with him? Bribe him with a wad of cash, and tell him to get lost and leave his girl alone? Punch him out? Perhaps a combination of all three? He didn't know, but as he told Scott and Anna to wait in the car, he thought he would soon find out. Whether he was there or not was irrelevant, either way, he had to get rid of him.

As it turned out, when he knocked on the door, it wasn't a man who answered, but a slight, pretty young woman with straight, glossy black hair in shortie pyjamas. Was this the right apartment?

'Hello. I'm looking for Cara St John. Is this the right place?'

The young woman opened her eyes and mouth, and eventually managed to sputter, 'Y-You are…you are…'

He was relieved to hear another, impatient voice come closer. 'For Heaven's sakes, Lucie! Who the heck is it? Either get rid of them or make them come in, but don't just stand there like a stunned mullet…!' Another woman came to the door, a bombshell peroxide blonde in a satin robe this time. When she saw Dan, she smiled a wickedly seductive smile and put a hand on her voluptuous hip. 'Oh. It's you. Come to see Cara, have you?'

'Yes!' he smiled, sighing with relief.

'Well, we're Cara's friends. This is Lucie, and I'm Pia.'

Dan extended his hand. 'Pleased to meet you. I'm…'

Pia took a hold of his hand, and yanked him into the apartment so hard he had to do a hop, skip and jump not to fall flat on his face.

'We know who you are,' Pia said, leading him into the living room. 'Cara talks about you all the time. Dan this, Dan that. Doesn't she, Lucie? Lucie?'

Lucie coughed. 'Oh. Yes. Definitely.' She signalled the lounge suite. 'Please, make yourself comfortable. Cara is in the shower, she'll be out in a moment.'

'Yes.' Pia sat very close to him, and looked him up and down. 'In the meantime, we'll have you all to ourselves. In the flesh. Although Cara never mentioned it was such magnificent flesh, I must say…'

Lucie grabbed a hold of Pia's arm, and with surprising strength for such a little person, pulled her up off the sofa. 'Pia, we really must get going. We've got a lot to do. Remember?'

'Remember what? It's Saturday, for goodness' sakes!'

'Remember the…' Lucie made rolling movements with her hands, raising her eyebrows at Pia '… the sponges?'

'Oh, yeah! The sponges!' Pia nodded.

Dan smiled, a puzzled look on his face. 'Sponges?'

'Yes,' Lucie nodded vigorously. 'See, I'm a caterer, and sometimes I get a big order for something…'

'…and she goes through loads and loads of sponges!' Pia interjected with a bright smile. 'Sponges for washing dishes, sponges for cleaning the benches and stove, sponges for mopping up spills, thick sponges, thin sponges, plain sponges, sponges with one side for scouring…you name it, she's got it. Sponges galore!'

Lucie opened her mouth to say something, then closed it. With admirable restraint, she thought for a moment, and when she finally spoke, it was as if to a child. 'Yes Pia, but the point is, I have to bake fifteen sponge *cakes*, and you said you'd help me. Right?'

'Oh! Right.'

Dan put a hand over his mouth, hiding his smile. They really were doing their best to come up with a good excuse to leave Cara and him alone. No matter that they were botching it up. If they wanted the two of them alone, it meant they were on his side, and that was a good sign. It must also mean that Robert wasn't here, so it was a doubly good sign at that.

'Well, it was nice meeting you.' He extended out his hand to both again as they left. 'Good luck with the…*sponges*.'

He sat back. Did Cara really talk about him all the time? And was this a good thing or a bad thing? *Ah well, it can't be too bad*, he thought, suddenly cheerful. If her friends want to leave us alone, maybe they know something I don't. He stretched his legs and, as he did, his foot kicked something under the edge of the sofa. He bent down to pick it up.

'Hellooooooo Carrot-top!' he murmured out loud. 'An empty bottle of chilli vodka! And to think you don't even drink.'

Sign number two that things weren't as dire as he'd

thought. His luck must be changing! And if it was the third time that was lucky, all he needed now was a third sign, and he'd be set.

As if on cue, the telephone suddenly rang. It seemed like such a cosmic coincidence that Dan looked heavenwards and gave it a thumbs-up. He could hear the shower still running, and so he knew it must be destiny. He picked it up.

'Hello, Cara St John's residence.'

'Hello? Who's this?'

Something about the insolent deep tone of the voice made little prickles of intuition make the hair on the back of his neck stand up. Could this be…?

'Well,' he said, giving his voice that subtle air of polite menace that the Mafiosi in the movies had, 'telephone etiquette decrees that it is the caller who must identify himself. So how about if you go first?'

Dan heard a sharp intake of breath and he had to bite his tongue to keep from laughing out loud.

'This is Robert Neville. Who the hell are you?'

'I'm Dan Hunter. And, Robert Neville, who the hell are *you*?'

Even after twelve hours, Cara's face still hurt and it was her own stupid fault. The strain of trying to keep a straight face through the first forty-five minutes of 'Mikhail McHale, Double Agent' had, she suspected, strained her jaw muscles. Just as well she hadn't tried to keep from laughing through the whole thing, she thought as she stepped out of the shower, or today she wouldn't have been able to open her mouth at all. After those first forty-five minutes, she hadn't been able to submit herself to that masochism any longer, and had let rip with a volley of snorting, hiccuping guffaws.

It really was very good. Dan had created a marvellous

composite character in Mikhail McHale, and most of the laughs came from the eighties action heroes he embodied. The plot was snappy, the espionage clichés exploited to the full, and Dan was in his element. He was a much better actor than she had expected, in a dual role as both Mikhail McHale and his evil nemesis, Herr X. There was a lot of cringing, self-conscious laughter from the audience, too, as they recognised the New Wave music and their old selves in the big hair and futuristic fashions.

It would be gratifying for Dan to see his movie do as well at home as it had overseas, and it would make his trip back home to Toongalla today an even bigger occasion. Good for him. He loved Toongalla and loved to visit, so at least one of them would have a good time.

Cara went back to Toongalla only when she had to, and then only briefly. Her childhood memories, Dan notwithstanding, were mostly happy, and she couldn't understand why she hated going back. Rather than feeling at home, in Toongalla she now felt like an alien. Toongalla was irrelevant to who she was now and she had blotted it out of her life so effectively that when she went back, she could hardly remember any of the people who recognised her down the street.

Heavens knew what she would do there! Follow Dan around, have several rare steaks rammed down her throat, and avoid the gossips, she supposed. Hardly her idea of a good time, but it was making a living. The main thing in all this, she must remember, was to avoid casualties. There were always casualties – of one sort or another – whenever she went back to Toongalla.

Damage control, she decided. She had better make sure the first casualty wasn't her, because the Toongalla gossips would have a field day when she and Dan turned up together. She would have to act, and look, like the perfect picture of professionalism.

Wrapped in a fluffy white towel, she grabbed an armful of the most suitable clothes for the weekend, and walked out into the living room.

'Hey, guys!' she called. 'Could you please help me choose something I can take this weekend that's casual but won't give anyone in Toongalla the wrong idea about why I'm there?'

'Well, what you're wearing right now certainly gives *me* the right idea,' Dan said from his vantage point on lounge suite.

Cara screamed, dropped the bundle of clothes, and held the towel around her so tightly it could have been a boa constrictor. 'Dan! What are you doing here? How did you get in?'

She was acutely conscious of all the bare skin she had on display and, apparently, so was Dan. The messages his eyes sent as they skimmed her body were like little pleasurable darts on her skin, stinging it into raised pinpoints of pleasure. She blushed as she remembered that only last night she had thought that the only thing that Dan's body should be dressed in was her own, and here it was on display, almost on offer for him! All he would have to do was cross the few steps towards her, tug on the towel, and...Boy, this apartment was hot! Delicate beads of sweat added to the moisture on her already damp skin, and she tried to think cool thoughts. *Deal with it*, she chastised herself. *We've already established he's attractive, but that doesn't mean you can go acting like a schoolgirl, melting into a hormonal puddle. You're an adult, now act like one!*

But if Dan's attractiveness was a threat, it was only a threat in her head. Dan wasn't coming towards her. As a matter of fact, other than enjoying her with his eyes, he was doing nothing much other than sitting, and cracking and eating the walnuts she kept on her coffee table with formidable bare hands.

'I came to pick you up.' He said. 'Your friends – Pia and Lucie, is it? – let me in. Nice girls.'

'Yeah, very nice. Where are they now?'

'They said they had to leave.'

Oh, she bet they had! *Well, they'll keep too*, she vowed.

'I see. Well,' she turned back to the bedroom, 'I'd better get dressed so we can get this show on the road.'

'Oh, before you go, Cara.' Dan cleared his throat. 'I just answered your phone.'

'Yeah?' Cara stopped in her tracks, instantly suspicious. 'Did you take a message?'

'Well, I couldn't, really. What he had to say was sort of…garbled.'

Cara felt that sense of impending doom once more. Funny how often she'd felt it since seeing Dan again. She looked at him suspiciously. 'Who was it, Dan?'

'Robert Neville. He said he was answering your call. Tried to get you all of last night, apparently.'

'Oh.' That was fine. Maybe the sense of impending doom had been a false alarm. 'Thanks, I'll ring him ba…'

'He wanted to know where you'd been. I told him you'd been with me.'

'You *what*?' The sense of impending doom was back, and getting stronger with every word Dan spoke.

'Well, it was the truth. He said, "Cara said she'd be working," and I said that if he didn't believe me, he could check the *Antipodean*'s weekend supplement.'

'Dan! I *was* working!'

'That's what I told him, but no matter what I said, after he saw the photograph, he found it hard to believe me.'

'What photograph?'

Dan held up the *Antipodean*'s weekend supplement, and Cara took it from him. There was an article on the 'Mikhail McHale, Double Agent' première, and a colour picture – rather a good one, she supposed – of her and Warren with their arms around each other's waists, smiling intimately at each other. She sighed and fell on to a chair. Warren had always been a lovely guy and a good friend, and she'd be forever grateful to him for getting her down that carpet, but this was just what she had been afraid of. Here she was, a serious journalist, crossing the line from professional distance into back-scratching territory. What a hypocrite she'd been, accusing Robert of selling out. It could have been a lot worse if Jenna Stephens and Ebony Jaxxon hadn't deflected attention away from her and Dan, but still, she and Robert would have to do a lot of talking to restore trust to their relationship.

'Oh, well,' she said flatly, 'at least it isn't a picture of me and you.'

'Maybe you should read the caption,' Dan said mildly.

Cara squinted at the writing, then opened her eyes wide.

Dan Hunter and his date for the evening, journalist Cara St John.

'I don't believe it! You and Warren look nothing alike! Well – not *that* much anyway. How could something like this happen?'

Dan leaned back and crossed his arms. 'Don't ask me.'

Cara peered at him. 'Dan…Dan, you *did* tell him it was a mistake, didn't you?'

'What do you take me for? Of course I did!' Dan was indignant. 'I told him that it was a mistake. "I have no idea how this could have happened," I said. "Cara says you work for a highly reputable paper", I said. "Cara says journalists for the *Antipodean* are above such mistakes," I said.'

'*Dan!*'

'What? It's all true!'

'But…the way you said it! Why didn't you call me so I could speak to him?'

'Well, I did offer. I asked Robert, "Would you like to speak about it with Cara?" He said he didn't realise you were there, and then I told him you were just getting dressed…'

Cara stood up, hands on her head. 'You told him I was getting *dressed*?' If Robert suspected that she'd crossed the line from professional to personal, then Dan had confirmed it!

'Well, it was the truth, as far as I knew. I mean, you can just imagine what he would have said if I'd told him you were wondering around the flat dressed in nothing but a towel!' Cara glared at him but said nothing. 'Anyway, that's when he got garbled. He said something about ethics and being the first to throw the stone, and giving in to the hottest date in town, and he mentioned someone called Heather who, apparently, is much better than you in bed. It didn't make much sense to me, but I told him I'd pass the message on.'

'No.'

Cara closed her eyes. That was it. It was over. Any hope there had been of fixing things with Robert and moving on to a new, better stage in their relationship was gone. And all for this stupid assignment, and a few careless remarks!

She opened her eyes, and saw Dan cracking walnuts with his bare hands, and tossing them back, one after the other. He was smiling. A self-satisfied sort of smile. Could it be…? He looked up at her then and, without a shadow of a doubt, with every atom of her brain, she suddenly knew. Those remarks had been anything but careless!

She pointed at Dan and began to move towards him. 'You...'

The look on her face made Dan stand up and begin walking backwards away from her advancing form. 'Is something wrong, Cara? You look upset...'

'Upset? Why should I be upset when someone who's just walked back into my life after fourteen years away decides what's best for me by getting rid of ...' What the heck was Robert again? '...of my lover?'

Dan swallowed hard. 'I didn't get rid of him. He came to his own conclusions. In a relationship, there has to be a large degree of trust and...'

'Trust? Let me tell you about trust. It is something I totally lack when it comes to you. Now tell me! You did it on purpose, didn't you? Didn't you!'

'I-I...'

Cara reached behind her and picked the nutcracker up off the coffee table. 'Own up, Dan, or I'll show you what I can *really* do with a nutcracker. And let me tell you, it won't be sweet.'

Dan was against the wall, Cara fast closing in. He put his palms up in front of him. 'OK! OK, I did.'

'I knew it!'

'Cara, you know why I did it!' He put his hands down and looked at her beseechingly. 'I want you. You and I belong together...'

The man was maddening! He had ripped her life to shreds in the course of just a few days, and now he was appealing to her sense of romance! A feeling of powerlessness and ire so strong that she thought she was going to explode pushed at her insides. She clenched her fists in front of her and screamed.

'Meant for each other? Let me tell you something,

Dan Hunter. I wouldn't have anything to do with you if we were stuck together on a desert island with only wild pigs for company! As a matter of fact, I would prefer the company of the wild pigs!'

She put her hands on her hips, breathing heavily, and glowered at Dan. Instead of looking upset, apologetic, defensive, or even cocky, his eyes and mouth opened as if he'd had a most brilliant idea. His mouth tilted up into a goofy crooked grin and Cara half-expected him to shout 'Eureka!' Talk about strange reaction from a potential lover spurned! Well, that was just typical. It reminded her a child who is deliberately naughty to get his parents' attention, and when he gets it in the form of a telling off, can't hide his delight, and so the parents have to say, 'Get that smile of your face!'

More attention seeking from 'The Ego That Took Over the World', and further proof of Dan's immaturity. Well – enough was enough. Dan must pay. Not only would he have to beg forgiveness on bended knee but he would also have to fix all the damage he and his rampaging ego had wreaked.

'Well?' she prompted. 'Have you got something to say?'

'Hmm? Oh yeah. Listen, I'll wait for you in the car, yeah? I've got a few phone calls to make.'

And with that he was out, and she was left standing, mouth open, arms limp at her sides. Unbelievable!

There was a knock at the door and Cara rushed to open it. 'Found some common human decency, have you? Well, this apology had better be goo…oh, it's you.' Cara visibly slumped as she let Lucie and Pia in.

'Gee thanks,' Pia said, 'nice to see you too.'

'Are you all right?' Lucie examined Cara's face. 'We saw Dan leave without you…'

'You saw Dan leave without me?'

Pia rolled her eyes. 'The peephole, of course. You didn't think we'd completely leave you to your privacy, did you? You'd have to be kidding!'

Cara wagged an index finger. 'Yeah, actually, I have to talk to you about that. Thanks to you, Dan has succeeded in giving my orderly, calm life the *coup de grace*. He's ruined everything!'

'Cara, what's happened?' Lucie sat down and pulled Cara down beside her.

Cara told them.

Lucie gasped and put a hand up to her mouth.

Pia threw her head back and laughed. And kept right on laughing.

'Pia!' Lucie admonished.

'Well, I can't help it! It's hilarious! I mean, Cara really needed to get rid of the creep, but this is so much better than "the talk". Ten out of ten for style, Dan Hunter.'

'What do you mean, I had to get rid of Robert?'

Pia made a dismissing movement with her hand. 'Oh, darling, it was a nowhere relationship.'

'What do you mean? I wouldn't be where I am today without him!'

Lucie cleared her throat. 'No one's disputing that, Cara. As a mentor, he was good – at the beginning, anyway – but…'

'As a lover, he stank,' Pia completed.

'*Et tu*, Lucie?' Cara shook her head. 'How can you say that? I can understand it from Pia, because he never liked her…'

'You listen to me,' Pia was now serious. 'I never wanted Robert to like me. As a matter of fact, if Robert ever did come to like me I'd consider my life well and truly over.'

'That's because you don't know him very well. If you were to spend time with him…'

'We don't need to spend time with him. We know him very well indeed, from the effect he's had on you.'

'Pia's right, Cara. You deserve better.'

Cara stood up. 'Better? Who's better? Dan?' Lucie and Pia shrugged, looked at each other, and then nodded their heads. Cara put her head in her hands and paced. 'Dan and I are terrible for each other! You want me to act out some crazy romantic fantasy, but this is real life, and it won't work. There is no common ground for us – we are two totally different people from two totally different worlds. He is all wrong for me.'

'And yet,' Lucie said softly, putting a hand on Cara's arm and pulling her back down again, 'since he's come back into your life, you have seemed more alive than you have in years. Like the Cara we first knew.'

'Alive?' Cara gasped. 'You call having to suffer my life being systematically dismantled being "alive"?'

'Sometimes, yes. If that's what it takes.'

'What it takes for what? My life was perfectly all right until he came along!'

'All right?' The look on Pia's face was incredulous. 'Your life was *all right*? Do you ever listen to yourself, Cara? And do you realise that it was actually Robert who systematically dismantled the life you had planned for yourself? Your dreams for a family, gone. Your self-respect in front of your peers, gone. Your ability to have a good time without intellectualising, gone. Hell, even the novel you've been writing as long as we've known you is gone as we knew it. You went from wanting to write a really good story to writing about *themes*, for heaven's sakes! And all at his insistence!'

'No, no…you've got it all wrong…'

Cara shook her head and got up, a hand over her mouth. It couldn't be true, could it? That her life had been constructed around this one man and his influence? She had always prided herself on her control. The thought that her control was nothing but a mirage left her feeling like she had just swallowed a bowling ball. Her life, not really her life, but someone else's idea of what it should be? The bowling ball refused to budge, and on some level she knew it was right. But…before Dan had turned up, she had been happy. Hadn't she?

She – like many people, she suspected – had always thought in terms of living a life that was either happy or unhappy. *Well,* she suddenly thought, *maybe that's too simple an interpretation. It's often easy to avoid being unhappy. Perhaps the trick to getting the most out of life isn't a matter of choosing good over bad, but of choosing best over something like* all right. Had she been settling for less? And if so, why?

She walked to the window and stared out at the sea, winking and beckoning under the bright light of morning. She felt a hand on her shoulder.

'Cara, are you OK?' Lucie asked.

Cara sighed. 'Yeah, but look, I don't want you guys blaming Robert, understood?'

'But, he's…'

'I don't care what he is,' Cara shook her head.

'Oh, jeez-louise, Cara!' Pia exclaimed. 'Don't defend the jerk!'

'I'm not interested in defending him! And I can't blame him either because that's taking the easy way out. What I'm doing is far harder.' Cara put a hand on her chest. 'I'm holding myself accountable.'

'Honey, you can't blame yourself.'

'It's not blame, Lucie, it's being a grown-up. See, even if he did exert all this influence over me, I still *let him do it*. At the end of the day, I'm responsible.' She paused. 'There had to be something in it for me, I'm sure. I've got to find out what it was, and why I let myself go along with him.'

'That's our girl.'

'Hey!' Pia called out. 'And when you find out what it was, you'll be free to run into Dan's golden, muscled arms, right?'

Cara smiled, but shook her head. 'Wrong. He still interfered and he's still responsible for that. I'm not going to let him off the hook so easily. Besides, no matter what I am, any fool can see that we're totally wrong for each other.'

'Oh, Caaaaraaaaaa!'

chapter nine

Cara had been silent all the way to Toongalla, but Dan wasn't going to yell this time. He'd got rid of that arrogant jerk, and good riddance. Even if it meant that she was going to give him the cold shoulder, it was still worth it. In time, Cara would see that he'd done her a favour, and she'd be grateful. She'd want to show her gratitude, and he'd be happy to see it…oh, yeah, he smiled to himself. It didn't matter that he was *persona non gratia* right now, and that she was looking out of the car window as morosely as if she were in an eighties music clip. In a couple of days, things would be different.

She'd have to speak to him, for a start. The silent treatment needs the right conditions and, after tomorrow, conditions would change. Talking to each other would be a necessity.

He'd be free from his entourage and commitments, and be free to feast on her with his eyes…and in other ways too! The thought was so hot that he had to send his brain – and other parts of his body – a quick 'Down, boy!' message.

But best of all, the trappings of their lives would be left behind. Just him, just her, left alone to rediscover what they had once shared.

It was the perfect plan. And who would have thought that Cara herself would have provided it for him?

'Cara, love!'

'Hello, Mum.'

Cara hugged her mother Patrizia, and kissed her delicate rosy cheek. Cara looked a lot like her mother, with the same creamy skin and flame-red hair that Patrizia had inherited from her Genoese family, but Cara thought she would never be as beautiful as her. It wasn't surprising that her father was still as passionate about his wife as he had been when he first sighted her in a sugar-cane field thirty-five years ago, sweaty from cutting alongside the men. He had travelled out to the fields with a photographer to do an article, but it had been instantly forgotten at the sight of Patrizia in her clam digger jeans and gingham shirt knotted just above her waist, hacking at the cane with a machete like an Amazon, flaming hair whipping about her face in the hot wind. James had conveniently lost the photographer, and found lightning-strike love, in one fell swoop.

'It's so lovely to have you back home. I'd almost forgotten what you look like!' She held Cara's face in her hands and then called out, 'James, Cara is here!'

Cara's father came out of his study pushing his glasses up his nose – they always slipped down when he was working at the typewriter – and then extended his arms for an embrace.

'Hey Dad,' she said when she'd been hugged, given the once over, and chastised for not having more meat on her bones. 'Do you think I could have some of your books? Autographed?'

'You? You want some of my books? Pat, am I hearing things? I could have sworn Cara said she wants some of my books.'

'Hmm. I thought I heard that too.'

'If I recall correctly, a certain 15-year-old once told me she was too old to read her old man's work, and would now exclusively read serious literature.'

'A second childhood, perhaps, James?'

'OK, OK,' Cara put her palms up in defence. 'I get the

point, thank you very much. Actually…' she paused and smiled a tight little embarrassed smile, 'They're not for me. They're for…a friend. A young girl. She's wonderful, Dad, and she loves your work…'

'Oh, well. I knew it was too much to hope that you'd begin to read my work again.'

Her father wasn't into guilt trips. His tone of voice was light and jovial, but it had a sad undertone that her conscience picked right up on and she thought, 'Casualty Number One: Dad.'

Cara looked down. An apology would be dishonest and patronising, because what he was saying wasn't exactly untrue. The fact was, she didn't respect his work and hadn't done so for many, many years. She still couldn't understand why he had turned away from a successful career in journalism to write – of all things! – children's books. He had begun writing them shortly after she was born, and could understand that the royalties from the books had helped make ends meet, but then to give up journalism altogether to write about make-believe? It didn't make sense, even when his children's books found considerable success. To Cara, it was inexcusable, a waste of talent. It was true, she had once loved the books – particularly the ones about Fiamma – but she had outgrown them and, deep inside, she felt that her father should have long outgrown them too.

James placed an arm around his daughter's shoulders and picked up her suitcase. 'Let me help you with your bags, and you can tell me all about this girl on the way to your room. I don't think you've had a young girl you could call a friend since you were one yourself, so that seems pretty newsworthy in itself. If she likes my books, that will be just as good.'

A bit of time spent unpacking, settling in, playing

with the dog, and then it was down to business as usual before a Toongalla party – making chocolate ripple cakes.

Everyone in Toongalla made chocolate ripple cakes, roughly put together with chocolate biscuits and whipped cream, but no one made them like Patrizia. Or Cara, who had watched and learned. Patrizia's version, flavoured with strong coffee and Amaretto, and mascarpone instead of cream, made children clap for joy, men beg, and women swoon. After a couple of hours of Cara and Patrizia's work, chocolate ripple cakes filled the refrigerator. A chocolate ripple cake wasn't something she would make for one of her dinner parties, but Cara had to admit, after sneaking a taste, that homely as it was, it was pretty darned good.

'Think that will be enough for the barbecue?' Patrizia asked.

'Oh, Mum,' Cara sighed and smiled indulgently. 'You always ask the same thing. You always worry there won't be enough food and, in the end, there's always too much.'

'There's no such thing as too much food. Someone always eats it.'

It was useless arguing. Her mother did not believe a leftover could ever be a waste. Piling disposable plates up with leftovers, swathing them in plastic wrap and pushing them into the willing hands of departing guests, was her idea of bringing a party to a successful close.

'So,' Patrizia said, beginning to wipe down the benches, 'How are things between you and Dan?'

Oh-oh, Cara thought, *here it comes. Now, what's the drill? I pretend I have no idea what she's hinting at, then she tells me exactly what she's hinting at, then I tell her she's crazy, and then she tells me I'm crazy*. Well, she was tired of it. For once, she would cut to the chase and put an end to it before she became casualty number two.

'Mum, there are no "things" between Dan and me. If you're talking about that picture in the newspaper...'

Patrizia made a dismissive movement with her hand. 'Oh, that picture. Anyone who knows the Hunters can tell that it's Warren and not Dan. What I meant is, well, you have been spending quite a lot of time with him, and I thought...'

'That your dreams had come true, no doubt.'

'Denise's too!' she exclaimed defensively and with charming honesty.

Cara smiled and shook her head. 'You're hopeless.'

'On the contrary, my dear darling daughter, I'm hope-*full*. Ever hopeful. You and Dan belong together. You always have, you always will.'

'No, we don't. It's pointless pursuing this, Mum! He and I are too different, and we just rub each other up the wrong way.'

Patrizia wagged a finger and gave her daughter a wicked smile. 'Oh, you should give him a chance, love. I know that if you did, you would find he can rub you up just the *right* way.'

'Mother! Behave yourself! You're a grown woman!'

'Yes, and believe me, as a grown woman, I know all about the different ways a couple can...rub each other. From the very first moment, I knew your father and I were right for each other, and I have known it about you and Dan too.'

'Mum, I'm sorry. You know I love you, and I appreciate that you want me to be happy, but you really don't *know*. You just...hope.'

'Well, Cara, I love you too, and I know the difference between knowing and hoping. I *know* you two belong together. And, God above, I *hope* you'll see sense one day soon and realise it!'

Her parents and the chocolate ripple cakes had already gone next door, and in her old room Cara could hear the happy buzz from the Hunter home next door as people arrived for the barbecue. If she knelt on her bed and stretched, she could see the Hunters' backyard.

The Hunter home was a ramshackle affair. It was beautifully kept, but nothing could detract from the skew-whiff air its four extensions had given it. Both Denise and Wayne had held that each child should have his or her own bedroom and, as the family had grown, so had the house. The Hunter home had grown out, then up, with extra rooms and bathrooms, a bigger kitchen, and finally a little haven upstairs to where Denise and Wayne could escape each night far from the madding crowd below. Luckily, the homes on Davey Street were on old quarter-acre blocks of land, and there was still plenty of room for the Hunter tribe to run and play outside, and eventually have their own pool.

There was Dan's bedroom window. With a nostalgic pang, she remembered how each of them would hang out of their windows, carrying yelled-out conversations that just couldn't wait until the next day. In those days, the two of them had lots in common, lots to talk about. What had they talked about? Nothing. The kind of nothing that to children means everything. No matter what her well-intentioned mother said, she and Dan didn't even have a fraction of what they'd shared as children but, even if they had, she was a child no longer, and needed far more than that.

The problem was…she couldn't quite pinpoint what she needed any more. She thought she had needed Robert and, painful as it was to admit, she didn't. She didn't love him, didn't need him as a mentor any more and, truth be known, she definitely didn't need him as a lover. A wave of heat emanating from the centre of her radiated out to the tips of her fingers and toes at the thought that Dan, with a mere touch, a kiss, had thrilled her, clothes on, standing up, a million times more than Robert ever had, naked, in bed.

No.

Cara gave herself an internal slap, trying to snap herself out of it. She didn't need Dan either. She didn't need his immaturity. His Hollywood-bred ego. His superficial job.

No, that wasn't right either.

She was doing Dan a disservice. He was more than that, she knew. He was perceptive, and sensitive, and loved kids, and was doing wonderful work as a Tich, and…darn it, why did things have to be so complicated! Things with Robert, they were simple. Robert was Robert. Robert was *safe*. And Dan…he was anything but safe. Robert was a Volvo on a quiet city street. Dan was a Ferrari on a winding mountain road. Breaking every speed limit. With no seatbelt on!

She didn't need that in her life.

The little voice in her head cleared its throat, and softly but clearly spoke up.

'When did you start thinking about needs, instead of wants?'

Cara sighed. This little voice was intent on making an appearance at the most awkward times, and there was nothing she could do but to answer it back so that it would shut up as soon as possible.

Because that's what being a responsible adult is all about. Putting needs above selfish wants.

'What – all the time?'

Yes.

'Not even if you want something so badly that you can't live without it?'

No such thing exists. There's nothing you can't live without.

'Yes, Cara, but at what cost?'

Cara bit her lip. At what cost indeed. She had been managing her life according to her needs instead of her wants and, at the end of the day, what could she say about it? That her life was *all right*. Not good, not great, not even awful – just this beige, lukewarm, *all right*.

But since Dan had come back…that was an entirely different story. What a roller coaster the last few days had been. The tingling anticipation of the climbs, the heart-stopping excitement of the heights, and stomach-leaping terror of the drops. And not one *all right* in sight.

But that was the problem with roller coasters. As much fun as they were, eventually the ride came to an end, and you had to put your feet on *terra firma* once more, leave the fairground, and go home. This was the reality. Whatever her wants or needs, there was too much water under the bridge.

In a few minutes, she'd have to go next door and face all their assorted friends and relations, field questions, defuse the explosive gossip, and subtly let everyone know that she had outgrown Dan. In fact, she had outgrown the entire town of Toongalla. So why did some part of her heart hum with childish expectation at the scene she could see unfolding next door?

Someone – probably Daria and Dalton – had strung up the backyard with a swinging canopy of paper lanterns, and candles and huge origami flowers floated in the swimming pool. In the back corner of the yard, there was a portable stage hung with strings of multi-coloured light-bulbs and the musicians, who had just had their glasses of beer replenished by Wayne, were warming up. Despite the band, despite the magical quality of the candle flames in the twilight, this was very much a family affair, down to earth, unpretentious. Typically Hunter. *Ah, what the heck*, Cara finally admitted to herself, *perhaps I haven't totally outgrown all of this. I love the Hunters, and I miss them.* But she wondered at the contrast between this and the life that Dan had created for himself in Hollywood. Shame.

Before going next door, Cara quickly surveyed herself in the mirror. In the aftermath of the disaster caused by Dan this morning, she had forgotten her resolve to wear something to the barbecue that would give people the right idea. She'd grabbed an armful of clothes from her wardrobe without looking, and although a couple of things had been suitable in her eyes, they hadn't been in Patrizia's. Everything was wrong, she had said. Almost everything Cara had packed was black, and her mother had to remind her that this was a country barbecue, not an *avant-garde* artist's funeral. Finally, Patrizia had approved a gauzy, colour-splashed top, and the only thing she could wear with it was an old pair of stretch jeans, circa 1986. Not quite what she had in mind to ease the gossiping, but Patrizia had pointed out that the gossips would be a lot more merciful if she just tried to blend in, for goodness sake!

As she walked out of the house, she took a deep breath and offered a silent prayer. *Please God, no more casualties*!

The shrill cacophony of the cicadas competed against the band, which was playing quiet mood music. The delicious aromas of the barbecue floated in the air, and as she breathed them in, Cara realised just how hungry she was. She decided to make an unobtrusive entrance and keep close to the fence, but as soon as she walked in through the gate, the old Misses Baker were on her, hanging on her arms, eyes glinting with the thrill of the hunt. The hunt for news they could share with all and sundry.

'Why, it's Cara! Ethel, it's Cara, isn't it?'

'Yes, Enid, it is. Cara, so nice to have you back in town again…'

'…and Dan, of course. Yes, Dan as well.'

'Did you come up here on your own, or…?'

'…together?'

Cara took a deep breath and fought to keep a toothy grin on her face. The Misses Baker were experts at interpreting all sorts of information, so that no matter what she said, they would spin something out of it. There was only one thing to do, and that was to never, ever, answer one of their questions.

'Hello, Miss Baker, Miss Baker. I'm afraid you'll have to excuse me. I have an ear infection and I'm finding it very hard to hear.'

Enid Baker raised her vibrato voice a few decibels.

'Ethel and I were wondering if you had come up here on your own, or together…'

'…with Dan,' her sister completed, louder than before.

'Oh!' Cara nodded and smiled as if suddenly understanding. 'With Wayne? No, I didn't. Wayne and Denise came back last night after the première, by plane. I came up this morning. Now, if you'll just excuse me…'

Cara escaped before they could protest, and looked ahead. It was like running a gauntlet! She decided that perhaps a discreet entrance wasn't such a good idea, and looking busy might work better. If she looked like she was on her way somewhere else, they might let her go. Taking a deep breath, she marched forth, shaking hands and kissing cheeks, briefly saying hello and then pointing to some indefinite spot beyond and excusing herself with a, 'Oh there's…I must…if you'll just excuse me…'

It worked until she came to a man who looked familiar but she couldn't quite place.

'Ray,' he said. 'Ray Coulter.'

'Ray…?' Cara repeated stupidly, then it came to her. 'Mr Coulter!'

When she had started attending Toongalla High, Mr Coulter had been an English and Humanities teacher but, within a few years had been promoted to Vice Principal. As a teacher, he had been the worst thing a teacher can be – uninspiring. As a Vice Principal, he had been the usual complement to a mild and inoffensive principal – a total thug. Whenever Mr Coulter would walk by, Dan would give him a Nazi salute behind his back, which she'd always silently applauded. *Oh dear*, she thought. She hadn't liked him then, she had no reason to like him now, and here she was being expected to call him by his first name, when her every instinct urged her to whip her arm up and shout, '*Heil, mein Fuhrer!*' But she was, after all, a grown-up, and grown-ups were masters of hypocrisy if nothing else. She gave Ray Coulter a blinding smile worthy of a toothpaste commercial.

'Ray, please. You remember me!' He smiled back proudly.

Let us forget! 'Of course. So – Ray – are you still at Toongalla High?'

'Yes, except I'm Principal now. How about you, Cara? Still at the *Clarion*? I must admit I wouldn't know – I find the *Clarion* a little too left-wing for my tastes.'

Cara bit her lip, but kept right on smiling. 'Yes, I am. I love working there.'

'Yes, it's wonderful for the town to see your name in the paper every day. And Dan! A world-famous entertainer, and everyone knows he's a Toongalla boy. We at

Toongalla High are very proud when our *alumni* get out there and make a difference.'

'But I'm sure all Toongalla High graduates are making a difference in the world, Ray, even if their names don't appear in the media,' she couldn't resist replying, albeit very politely.

'Oh, yes, of course,' Ray said dismissively, 'but at the end of the day, it's people like you and Dan that our youth look to for an example, not the ones selling insurance or having children.'

Cara looked down, thinking of the parents of the children she'd met at the Brisbane Children's Hospital. Once a thug, always a thug. The thuggery techniques might have changed, but the attitudes that drove them obviously hadn't.

'Well,' she finally said, 'it seems to me that you are underestimating the children. And you never know – if society were to put parents or decent people on pedestals as we do people in the public eye, maybe our children would have better role models. Perhaps there'd be fewer girls starving themselves to look like supermodels, or boys committing suicide because they can't measure up.'

Ray looked at her, eyes wide open for a split second, then threw his head back and laughed. 'Oh, Cara, I see you haven't changed!' *Neither have you, Herr Coulter*, she thought. 'But surely you're not saying that you wouldn't want a child to be inspired by your example?'

'Of course not. What I actually meant was…'

'Good. Well, why don't you come to the school on Tuesday? We have invited Dan to speak to the students, as we feel he'd be an inspiration to them. An address from you beforehand would be a wonderful prelude to it, I think. Can you be in the school auditorium at ten?'

Damn it, of course she could. Tuesday was her last day

with Dan, and where he was, she would be too. Oh well, she sighed to herself, if she couldn't get out of it, she would make sure she was a more realistic model for the Toongalla High kids than Dan was. She might only be a prelude to the main speaker, but she would make a difference if it killed her.

'Ten o'clock is fine. See you then.'

Her mother and Denise were setting bowls of salad on a table already buckling under the weight of laden platters.

'Cara, darling! I was just telling your Mum what a lovely time we had together yesterday, shopping and whatnot. Such fun.'

Yeah right, fun for you, Cara thought, but merely nodded and smiled, stealing a carrot stick from a plate of crudités and crunching on it viciously.

'Do you want Dan?' Patrizia smiled.

'Me?' Cara choked on the carrot. 'No! Why would I…want Dan?'

Patrizia and Denise gave each other subtle smiles, then Patrizia turned back to address her daughter. 'You're doing a piece on him, remember?' she said in an overly gentle, motherly tone. 'A week in the life, wasn't it? Or do we have it wrong?'

The two women weren't laughing out loud, but Cara could see them laughing on the inside. They were loving it! They loved her defensiveness and her blushing, and the fact that she and Dan were manacled to each other for the week. She gave them a look that told them she knew exactly what they were thinking.

'No, Mother, you don't have it wrong. See?' She pulled out a pad and pencil from her back pocket. 'I've even brought these. And, by the way, they're for work, not for playing tic-tac-toe. Just so you remember, I *am* a grown-up.'

'Whatever you say, darling.' Denise put a hand on her arm. 'He's playing cricket down the other side of the house.'

Cara thanked her and walked away, but before she was out of earshot, she heard Denise say – on purpose, she was certain – 'What an oversensitive girl.'

'Yes,' Patrizia nodded vigorously, also loud enough for her to hear, 'and you know what they say. You are only oversensitive when someone hits the nail on the head, aren't you? Now, if you ask me…'

Cara clenched her fists at her sides and walked towards the side of the house. She could hear the knock of willow on leather and the scramble of many feet, and the whoops and laughter of children, cheering and throwing friendly insults at each other. Rounding the corner, she saw Dan, up to bat in front of a garbage bin wicket, surrounded by assorted nieces and nephews and friends' children, totally a part of them. In the eternally sexy uniform of a pair of well-worn jeans and a white T-shirt that hugged his formidable torso, he looked very much a man, but his playful abandon was a complete contrast. Something within her warmed at the sight of him, so refreshingly unguarded, and she shook her head. Almost all her life she had criticised him for being so childish, and here she was, going goggle-eyed at the sight of it! But no, it was more than that, she suddenly realised. He actually had a child-like quality, and that was a different thing altogether. Good for him – he needed it for his Tich work. She admired people who could tap into that part of themselves, but she couldn't.

Ah well, back to Dan, and back to work, she thought. She made a note on her pad, dictating it to herself as she wrote, 'Dan Hunter loves children.' Actually, it was a mooter-than-moot point after the scenes in the children's hospital and, as she looked around to see if anyone had seen her writing, she bashfully had to admit to herself that she'd done it to show everyone at the party she was there to do her job.

She sighed, suddenly feeling quite alone. For a moment in her room, she had looked forward to this, but now that she was there, she was forced to face the ever-present reality that she did not belong in Toongalla. No one here cared about her life. They only cared about her life in terms of what they could relate to, here in their own small world. She didn't care what they thought, not really, but it would have been nice to be appreciated and admired just for herself – not for how it reflected on the town.

Much as Dan was her total opposite, and much as she would hold him responsible for his crazy behaviour that morning, right now he was the closest thing to her life in Brisbane. As she watched him jump up and down in victory with several children hanging off him, hair tumbling around his laughing face, she wished he would look up and restore the link she needed to feel. But he was so absorbed in his play that there was no way even a telepathic connection would have worked. She walked away.

Mingling was a nightmare. Having conversations without giving much of yourself away was impossible, and she eventually gave up. Instead, she found herself a seat in a far corner next to the jasmine and, leaning her head back against the sweet blossoms, she closed her eyes and hoped for a time warp effect that would bring this weekend to an end as soon as possible. Or if not a time warp, a nice little alien abduction would do! She was already an alien in Toongalla, anyway, and if a flying saucer came and took her away, it would be much of a muchness. But without the stress.

'Charred animal flesh?'

Startled, Cara opened her eyes, and found a plate piled with food being pushed under her nose. It was Dan, flushed and gleaming from the cricket game, making the offer with one of his beautiful smiles, all four dimples on display. *Damn it*, she thought as her heart did a perfect flip that would have earned a gold medal in the Olympics, *he really is gorgeous. Not handsome, not sultry, not brooding-good-looking, but gorgeous*. He had that boyish quality that appealed to young girls, as well as the kind of women who liked to mother a guy, but he was unmistakably all man. His dark brows, in striking contrast with his blond hair, could make his eyes change from playful to smouldering, and every other emotion that he needed to display as an actor, and he had the most kissable mouth she had ever seen – or, indeed, kissed. His top lip was perfectly curved, and just as the button on a cushion draws attention to the cushion's plumpness, so did the dividing line down the middle of his lower lip draw attention to its fullness. She could imagine licking at that lower lip, indeed exploring all that mouth and its little points of interest, at length and with great pleasure. *Yep, no doubt about it*, she thought as she willed away another internal heat wave, *he is drop-dead gorgeous*. She knew it, she knew he knew it, and they both knew millions of sane and normal females around the world knew it. That she was the same as them didn't make her feel any better about it.

'Pat made me promise, on my life, to bring you a steak.'

'But I don't…' she began to protest.

'Eat red meat. Yeah, I know. She went on and on about it. But see, I also brought a tandoori chicken breast. She didn't say I had to make you eat the steak, did she? So let's share the plate – I'll have the steak, you have the chicken, and no one will be any the wiser,' he finished, handing her a knife and fork wrapped in a white paper napkin.

She cleared her throat. Share a plate! In two seconds flat, her mother and Denise would translate sharing a plate to sharing a bed and then she'd never hear the end of it.

'Thanks, but no thanks.'

Dan signalled with his head to a point just behind her. 'Oh, come on, Cara. Miss Baker and Miss Baker are watching. If they don't see you eat, they'll go from assuming you're anorexic, to assuming you're pregnant, in one fell swoop.'

Cara turned around. The Misses Baker really were watching! So – she had to choose the lesser of two evil rumours. Mum and Denise she could handle, at a pinch. But the Misses Baker? Not even an expert at defusing explosives could handle the Misses Baker. She sighed and gave Dan a crooked smile.

'OK. Just so long as you don't expect me to talk to you or anything.'

'Why not? You're not still angry at me about that little thing this morning, are you?'

'Little thing? Ha!' she exclaimed. 'You interfered in something that was none of your business! You can expect me to be angry for quite a while, thank you very much. You crossed the line, Dan. I mean it, what you did was no joke.'

Dan put down the plate of food and rested his forearms on his thighs, fingers interlaced. He cast his head down, and Cara wondered what he was preparing to say. *Maybe even a comic genius mind needed time to think up a smart retort sometimes*, she thought. But when he looked up, his face was subdued and earnest.

'I'm sorry, Cara.'

Cara narrowed her eyes, and peered at him closely. If

she wasn't mistaken, he meant what he was saying! He really, actually meant it.

'You're serious.'

'Yeah, I'm serious. Why are you so surprised? Don't you think I have a serious side?'

'No.'

Dan shook his head and his eyes were so piercingly earnest that she felt pinned by them.

'But I do. I'm serious about the things I care about. My work with sick kids. My family.' He paused, and Cara held her breath, instinctively knowing he was about to dunk her in the deep end yet again. 'You.'

chapter ten

'Dan!' Startled, Cara quickly shook her head. It wasn't fair of him to do this, not here in Toongalla, where there was no escape. 'This isn't the right time…'

Dan leaned forward. He didn't touch her, but his closeness was enough to get her nerve-endings humming.

'It's never the right time for you and I, Cara! It wasn't right when I was a zitty adolescent who only knew how to make you react – even if it wasn't the kind of reaction he dreamed about in secret. It wasn't right when you were in Year 12 and I thought that maybe if you got to know another side of me, we could start again. And it's not right now, not when there's this Robert guy in the picture.' He looked down, almost boyish in his awkwardness, and Cara's heart spilled over with emotions she couldn't even begin to analyse, making her eyes pool with tears. 'I love you…'

'Please, Dan, don't…'

'No. Let me say it, even if you don't want to hear it or believe it. I love you. I have never, ever, loved anyone else but you, and I will never, ever love anyone else but you. Whatever I've done, whatever I do, you have to believe it's because I love you. And because I love you, I have to accept that you might prefer this jerk, Robert Neville, to me. And so…' he shrugged painfully and bit his lower lip, '…if you want, I'll go and ring him right now and set him straight. I'll tell him I gave him the wrong idea on purpose, and that you…you…love him very much?' These last few unsure words were torn out of him, as if putting the thought into actual speech had been a Herculean effort.

He was talked out, and Cara's brain was exhausted. She had no thoughts – just felt an injection of something warm and sweet directly into her veins. That and an overwhelming urge to run her fingers down the side of Dan's gorgeous face, and maybe comb them through his golden hair. If her heart had done gymnastic flips before, then now it had its arms raised in victorious Olympic salute, basking in the applause of a million hormones.

'Well, I'll be, Dan Hunter. I believe you really are sorry.' She finally sighed, a forgiving smile lightening her features. She paused, then looked down briefly. 'But there's no need for you to ring Robert up. You're right about him jumping to his own conclusions. And you're wrong about me loving him.'

Dan's own face brightened with a smile of joy and relief, and he flung himself back against the backrest of his chair, letting out an almighty sigh. 'Oh, thank God.'

Cara brought an index finger up in warning, trying hard not to smile. 'But don't go thinking that it leaves the way clear for you and I, or anything like that, understand?'

'No, ma'am!'

'Good. Now why don't you go and mingle with the guests?' she smiled, hoping the smile looked sincere. In fact, Cara was deeply shaken, and needed some space between her and Dan. For all of Dan's light-heartiness, time spent around him was intense. It drained her of all the energy she usually spent on thinking, leaving her vulnerable to an onslaught of feelings, physical and emotional, that she had no defence against. Dan's declaration of love – well, it had scared her. But not as much as her reaction to it. That viscous, warm, honey-like substance that seemed to have replaced her blood still coursed through her system, her heart beating extra hard, extra loud, to cope with the strain. She needed him to leave, or…what? What would she do? Fling herself into his arms and cling to him like a limpet on steroids?

Probably, that little voice inside her head said, *Because Dan is not what you need, but he's definitely what you want, isn't he?*

Oh, God help her, he was. He was! It had been easy to deny when they had just met again at the start of the week, but since then, he had not only turned her world upside down, but he was successfully removing, one by one, all the reasons why she had kept him at arm's length. She said he was superficial, he proved he wasn't. She said he was a product, he proved he was flesh – luscious, beautiful flesh – and blood. She said he was attractive only to star-struck teenagers, and he proved her so wrong that Cara's every molecule now screamed 'Sex, thy name is Dan Hunter!' every time he was near. And just now, he had proved that he could be serious when it mattered, when there were fragile feelings at stake. Looking at him now, a soft, playful smile on his face as he regarded her, head cocked to the side, it was easy to believe she could have her cake and eat it too, without the cholesterol, indigestion, or weight gain.

'You're a guest. Why can't I mingle with you?' he said. 'You look so miserable, and I'd be a really bad host if I didn't make sure you had a good time.'

'Well, actually, you're not the host. You're the guest of honour.'

Dan threw his head back and laughed. 'Guest of honour? Me? In my own home? If I were to even suggest such a thing, the family would have my guts for garters, and Danielle would be wearing them. Now – tell Doctor Doody what the problem is and I'll see if I can make it better.'

'It's nothing really,' Cara smiled and shrugged. 'The party is lovely, but it's…' *It's you, Dan Hunter*, she wanted to say. *It's you, messing with my mind, and my heart, making me wonder whether I dare to want something so very, very dangerous.* But she couldn't say it. If she did, he would step in and remove the decision from her, and she would be lost, lost to everything and everyone, including herself, and she wouldn't reappear until it all came to an inevitable end and she was left to clean up the damage. She cleared her throat. '…Toongalla. I always feel stressed out when I come here, not to mention out of place.'

'Ah.'

'You can just slot right back in, but I can't do that. My life is so different to this…' Dan chuckled, interrupting her philosophising. 'What are you laughing at?'

'Sorry, but that's funny. How similar do you think *my* life is to this?'

He had a point.

'Not much, I suppose. So, how do you do it?'

Dan shrugged. 'I don't know what it's like for you but, when you're famous, every time you meet someone new, you begin to wonder what they want from you. Believe me, it either drives you nuts, or you end up in a mansion behind high, electrified fences with nothing but servants and a chimpanzee for company. There's got to be a place, and there's got to be people, that you can be totally unguarded with.' He looked around at the gathering of old friends and family, and smiled. 'For me, that's Toongalla.'

'But don't you think everyone here wants something from you too?'

'Sure they want something from me! The Misses Baker want some juicy gossip, Mr Tomlinson wants me to take his daughter out on a date, and Blakey wants the contents of my wallet. But what they want now is exactly the same as what they wanted from me before I was famous. By and large, in Toongalla, we can all trust each other.'

'Well, I feel like they want something from me too, and even though I have no idea what that is, I'm 100 per cent certain I'm not giving it to them.' The conversation seemed to have steered away from dangerous ground, and Cara felt relaxed enough to pop a piece of the spicy, smoky chicken in her mouth. 'But there's more to it than that. I'm just never at ease, and I don't know why.'

'It might help if you lightened up a bit. Relax and have some fun!'

'Yeah, well, Dan, I don't think your idea of fun is the same as mine.'

'Nonsense. Here – the new band is coming on. And I bet you won't be able to resist having fun with me.'

Cara turned around. The first musicians had left and were being replaced by a seven-piece band in sharp suits and porkpie hats. The lead singer grabbed the microphone and pointed at the Cara and Dan.

'Hey, you!' he called out in a Cockney accent, 'Don't watch that, watch this!'

The singer continued the famous introduction to the song, 'One Step Beyond', and Dan leaned over to her.

'They're a Madness cover band called 'All in The Mind'. I remember how much you used to love Madness, and I knew you wouldn't be able to keep still.'

'What – you got the band for me?'

'Well…' he smiled, '…partly. They're a great band, so I knew everyone would like them, but mostly I wanted to see if I could shake you out of that uptight state you're usually in.'

'Who's uptight?'

'You are.'

'I am not!'

'Then prove it. Come on, let's dance – I dare you to start a Nutty Train.'

'I've forgotten how,' Cara mumbled.

'Yeah, right. Now you've got two choices – get up and dance with me, or stay here and talk to me about what's *really* eating you. And you know I can drag it out of you. You know I will.'

Cara bit her lip, the slight sting only slightly deflecting the thrill his words sent to her. Those threats Dan had, threats that sounded like dangerous, exciting promises, really were something. And they were something to take seriously, she realised that now. He was very perceptive and persuasive. She had no doubt that he could drag what really was the matter out of her – although in actual fact, dragging was too violent an image. He could coax open the door to her secrets with the sensitive, delicate fingertips of a master safe-cracker...

That image was also thrilling enough to bring fresh colour to her cheeks. No, this would definitely *not* do. *Keep it light, keep it light*, she told herself. *Be pleasant, and try to lighten up, and maybe, just maybe, he'll be shocked enough by your uncharacteristic behaviour that he'll leave you and your secrets alone.*

She looked up and managed to give him a careless smile.

'Well, I must say, Dan, if music is supposed to be the soundtrack of your life, then Madness is exactly the sort of music to have when you're around. You're on!'

The two moved to the dance area as the band launched into the frenzied beat of 'One Step Beyond', horns blaring, bass thrumming, and saxophone wailing out the tune, the organ making it sound like a fairground on acid. This was music to have fun to and Dan and Cara eased into long-unused dance steps as if they had never been forgotten. Others joined in, and Cara kicked off her shoes as they began working up a sweat.

'Think I can't start a Nutty Train? Just watch!'

As the music became more and more lively, Cara gathered everyone around. After a brief demonstration, accomplished despite everyone's incredulous laughter, they joined in, marching along in a line behind her with legs bent, arms pumping like crank pins. Then there was a final shout and a deafening clangour as the seven musicians thumped on their instruments for an end that would have raised the roof if there had been one. Cara collapsed against Dan, laughing and panting. She had forgotten all about Madness, and dance music, and how much pure, unadulterated fun it could be.

'I haven't done that in years! I'm exhausted!'

'I thought as much. But tired already? I'd say that, despite that gorgeous slim body of yours, you are very unfit, young lady.'

'Well, we can't all afford a personal trainer, you know.'

'Personal trainer? I'll have you know this is all naturally occurring!'

'Yeah, and so is this.' She poked her tongue out at him.

'Cheeky girl,' he murmured, and his gaze rested on her moist lips as she put her tongue away. Suddenly the mood changed, and the air around them seemed to fizz and crackle with a power that Cara knew could set her smooth hair on end. The band struck up another song, but despite being right in front of the amplifiers, Dan and Cara stayed where they were, in a world of their own.

Finally Dan smiled and cleared his throat. 'I'm... thirsty.'

'Me too.'

'Drink?'

'Yes, please.'

'Let's go.'

They were making their way to the drinks table ntly, walking very close, when suddenly Dan came to nplete standstill, a strange look on his face.

'What is it?'

'Look who's just arrived.' Dan nodded his head towards the gate, and Cara looked. It was Brian Hutchence, carrying two bottles of red wine.

'Hutch! I didn't know he was coming.'

'Well, of course Mum and Dad invited him. He wasn't just your Uncle Hutch, if you'll remember.'

'It's good he's here. I need to let him know how the article is coming along.'

Cara began to march towards him, but Dan's firm grip on her arm stopped her.

'No. This will be far more interesting.' He elbowed her in the ribs and nodded to the other side of the yard, where Anna was having an intense conversation with Ray Coulter. 'Take a look.'

Anna was in the middle of a highly gesticulated speech, when she suddenly saw Hutch and stopped in the middle of what she was saying, mouth open, arms akimbo. After a split second, she excused herself from Ray and resolutely made her way towards Hutch.

'This might be a good time to point out that Hutch and Anna met about twelve years ago in Washington during the presidential election,' Dan smiled. 'Hutch was covering it and Anna was on the campaign team. She told me about it just the other day, and the gleam in her eye seemed to suggest that the fireworks weren't just confined to the White House.'

Cara was amazed. It was a small world all right, but this news was unexpectedly fortuitous. If the barracuda-like Ms Di Vito ever questioned her professionalism again, Cara would just mention Hutch and wink knowingly.

With an unsettling smile, Anna closed in on Hutch. Cara and Dan saw Hutch narrow his eyes in confusion, then widen in recognition. Oh, this was good.

Dan elbowed her in the ribs again. 'Come on, let's eavesdrop.'

'I couldn't!' she whispered out of duty to Hutch, but her heart wasn't in it.

'Of course you can. You know you want to.'

He took her hand and they sneaked closer, first hiding behind a column, then behind a group of people laughing raucously at a string of progressively dirtier jokes, and then behind the fern house. From there, Dan and Cara peeked out, straining their ears to listen.

'...and I'm here until Wednesday. Anyway,' Anna was saying, 'under this Donna Karan dress, I'm wearing a black, shiny ciré teddy from Frederick's of Hollywood. It's a cross between a classic and dominatrix style, with a thong back. I'm wearing a power half-slip from Frederick's as well. I find I can't be seen in public without some lycra on my thighs these days, not since the lipo I had done a few years ago. Against my better judgement, I might add. Someone suggested I have some fat vacuumed out of my butt and I did. As it turns out, the fat made a reappearance on my thighs, and no matter how much I starve myself or do Tae-bo it seems it's there to stay...'

Cara and Dan listened on, mouths and eyes agape in fascinated horror, and saw their look reflected on Hutch's face as perfectly as if he had been a mirror.

'Dan?' Cara whispered. 'Dan, you know what Anna's doing, don't you? She's...'

'...coming the raw prawn with Hutch!'

Dan leaned over to Cara, who was sitting on the aqua-blue seat, staring hypnotically into the yacht's wake. He was beginning to panic. Why on earth would she agree to going ashore to Cobaar Island with him when she hadn't even wanted to talk to him all morning?

'Silence so thick, you could cut it with a knife,' he whispered.

Cara looked up and glared at him. 'What do you expect? Look at her, she's absolutely mortified!' she whispered back.

Dan turned to look at Anna. Rather than blushing, stuttering, or wishing to disappear into the floorboards, Anna's particular brand of mortification entailed small acts of violence towards thankfully inanimate objects. After the raw prawn fiasco, she had busied herself by helping out with the party. She had barbecued and speared sausages so viciously that every man had winced at the sight, and then had scrubbed the pattern off the dishes she had washed. Now she was sitting apart from everyone else on the yacht, busying herself by ripping the labels off all the champagne bottles, and tearing them into small pieces. When there were no more labels, she started on the paper napkins.

Poor Anna, Dan thought. But if he had learned anything about her, it was that she was a tough cookie. In time, she would see the humour in the situation and, if she didn't, well, she would still survive. If she hadn't re-ignited *the thing* between her and Hutch by reciting her underwear inventory, who was to say it had needed – or wanted – re-igniting in the first place? Or indeed, that it couldn't be re-ignited in some other way? So why Cara was acting so indignant on Anna's behalf, he would never know.

'Well, I understand why *she's* giving me the silent treatment. Now the question is, why are *you* giving me the silent treatment?'

'You did an awful thing to Anna! You totally misled her about what it means to come the raw prawn! When she went up to Hutch, she honestly believed we Australians greet each other that way!'

Dan chuckled incredulously. 'Excuse me, Ms Righteous, but I do believe I did it to save your cute little red-suspender-clad bum! Your own behaviour in coming the uncooked crustacean with me, as it were, required some quick explanation. From what I recall, you were grateful.'

'Still – you could have explained it all to her later on!'

'Why? She's got a Dinkum Dictionary. She could have looked up the meaning of coming the raw prawn or the uncooked crustacean, or whatever, before trying it out with Hutch, and found out for herself that it means "don't pull my leg"!'

'That's no excuse! Besides, you talked me into eavesdropping, which was…'

'Ha! Since when do journalists need to be persuaded to eavesdrop? You were dying to listen in, and both you and I know it.'

'I was not!'

'You were so!'

'Was *not!*'

'Were so!'

The argument exhausted, Cara and Dan stared at each other, then turned their heads towards at Anna.

At that moment, she looked up from her formidable pile of paper napkin confetti straight at them. With her dark sunglasses and unfathomable expression, she could have been The Terminator. Dan could imagine the view from behind Anna's sunglasses as she observed them. Their petrified forms would be right in her sights and beeping, computerised words would appear beneath them: *Dan Hunter and Cara St John. Target status: Expendable!* And here they were, on a yacht, in the middle of the deep blue sea, with no escape. Dan gulped. When Anna got back to the States, he'd better have a really expensive gift awaiting her.

He cleared his throat and turned back to Cara. 'So, how are you enjoying the outing?'

Although Wayne had a much-loved boat, it was just a fishing runabout that would have only fit six people maximum. For this outing, and his plan, Dan had needed something bigger, and his old school friend Peter Marx had come to the rescue. The 'Star of the Sea' was Peter's beautiful yacht, and he had agreed to help carry out the plan for the princely sum of one bottle of single malt whisky and autographed glossies for his daughters.

Peter had sailed out of Toongalla Bay into the open sea, and over a refined and well-lubricated lunch had then followed the coast, taking them into sheltered coves and around several islands, some populated, some not. It was a glorious day, and Dan would have been enjoying it if it weren't for the fact that he had a necessary, albeit devious, plan to carry out. He had hoped Cara would be in a better mood to be receptive to it, but looking at her after he asked the question, he knew it was a hard task.

'Don't try to engage me in conversation.' She lifted her chin and looked out to sea. 'I'm not talking to you.'

'But Cara, I…'

'Not another word.'

'Really, Cara…'

'If you don't stop talking to me right now, I'll do what I used to do when I was ten-years-old, and start humming.'

'OK, fine!'

'Fine!'

Dan shook his head and stood up. She was on her hobby horse again, on her way to heavens knew which crusade now. Without her co-operation, it was a whole new ballgame.

'Hey Peter,' Dan said, poking his head into the cabin, 'guess what. Cara's giving me the silent treatment again and there's no way she's going to want to be alone with me.'

Peter grinned like a boy with a crate of fireworks and a box of matches. 'Well, there's nothing for it then. Let's put Plan B into action.'

'Are you sure everything will be all right?'

'Listen – everyone's been filled in, and everything's ready and waiting for you. Don't pike out on us now. Faint heart never won fair lady, you know.'

Dan sighed. 'Yeah, I know. I just hoped it wouldn't come to this.'

'It'll be fine. Now, you go back to Cara, and just leave everything to us.'

Dan went back to his seat beside Cara, giving everyone he passed a significant look. He hoped everyone would be OK – particularly Anna. He had no way of knowing what she was thinking behind those dark glasses, but as a woman wronged, she was a dangerous quantity. If she wanted to, she could put not just a spanner but an entire tool belt into the works.

He didn't have to wait long for Peter to come out of the cabin.

'Everyone, if you could please pay attention? We have a small problem. It seems the boat is taking in water.' The look on Peter's face was appropriately worried, but he spoke with a curious monotone. *I hope Cara assumes it's shock and not just ham acting*, Dan thought.

At Peter's announcement, there was a chorus of fairly convincing indrawn breaths and exclamations, and Dan sneaked a look at Cara. She had stood up and was holding on to her glass of lemonade fit to shatter it. The trap was set.

Wayne cleared his throat. 'Oh! Oh, this is…er…indeed a calamitous predicament we find ourselves in. So, Peter, umm…what are we to do now?'

Oh, man, Dad's acting is far worse than Peter's! Dan glanced at Cara again, and saw that she was biting her lip. If she knew that this was a performance, she probably would have burst out laughing by now.

'Well, the water isn't coming in too fast. We could probably make it back to the mainland but I would rather err on the side of caution. I've already placed a distress call to Ocean Rescue and given them our co-ordinates. They advised us to abandon ship.'

This time Cara spoke, just one, strangled word. 'What?'

'Don't worry, Cara,' Peter smiled reassuringly, and pointed starboard. 'We're just a hop skip and jump from Cobaar Island. The dinghies will get us there without any problems, and we can safely await rescue there.'

Cara frowned and shook her head. 'Rescue,' she murmured to herself. 'He actually said, "rescue". I don't believe it.'

'OK, everyone!' Peter called. 'Follow me!'

Everyone moved towards Peter, who started handing out lifejackets, but Cara stayed put. *Oh, no*, Dan thought in dismay. *She said she didn't believe it. Perhaps she meant she didn't* believe it. He sighed. Time to come clean, and to hell with it. It had been a stupid idea, anyway.

'Cara,' he said, coming close and grasping her shoulders, 'I'm sorry…'

'Yeah, and so you should be. This is only the latest in a long line of disasters since you came into my life again! And although things seemed pretty bad after you got rid of Robert yesterday, being shipwrecked really takes the cake!'

Dan bit his lip to keep from smiling. All was well! 'What – you're going to hold me responsible for the yacht going down as well?'

Cara put her hands on her hips. 'Well, as it happens, it's dawned on me that quite apart from the Godzilla tactics you've employed on my life, you are also a jinx! Let's just say that, at this point of my time with you, I'm not surprised that the boat we're both on is sinking. And don't think that the symbolic meaning of it has escaped me, either.'

With that she marched off, and Dan followed, head hanging to hide the grin that finally escaped his bitten lips.

'Right,' Cara said, clicking on the belt of her lifejacket and leaning over the side, 'let's get this show on the road.'

She was greeted by embarrassed apologies from Denise, Wayne, James, Patrizia, Scott and Anna, bobbing in the inflatable dinghy on the calm blue water below.

'Sorry, love, we're all full up,' Patrizia called up with a motherly smile.

'Yeah,' Peter cleared his throat, 'It's a six-person dinghy, I'm afraid. You'll have to go in the other dinghy with Dan…'

Cara looked up, first at Peter, then at Dan, and then back at Peter again. She held her hands up in front of her and shook her head.

'Oh, no. No! No way am I going in a dinghy with the jinx from hell. Hey, Dad!' she called below, 'Whatever happened to "women and children first"? I'm your child, aren't I?'

'Well, actually, darling,' James was finding it very hard to keep the amusement out of his voice, 'you're always at great pains to point out that you are a grown-up, not a child. Now you be a big girl and go in the dinghy with Dan. You'll be fine.'

Anna took her sunglasses off and laughed. 'Yeah. Just remember if you get stuck on an island with Dan, to stay away from those raw prawns.'

Just watch it, Anna, Dan thought, but Cara was beyond finding any significance in the comment. She clenched her fists and looked up at him through eyes arcing sparks.

'I don't believe it! My own father! And Anna laughing at me, all because of you!'

Dan appealed to Peter with a silent, desperate look, and Peter rolled his eyes.

'Now then, Cara, just calm down,' Peter said, taking hold of her arm. 'You can't go in the dinghy with the others, you'll compromise their safety…'

'Fine, so I won't go in. I'll stay in the water and hold on to the side. I'm going over!'

'Cara, no!'

Cara lifted her leg over the rail and leaned over the side. Dan and Peter lunged and grabbed at her, and began to pull her back into the boat.

'Let go of me!' she bit out through teeth gritted with exertion.

'No!'

'I said, *let…go*!'

With that, she yanked her body out of their grasp. The laws of physics decreed that the two men go with their momentum, and they hit the deck flat on their bums. The force of Cara's sudden, new-found strength however, also yanked her out of the grip she had on the yacht. With an ear-splitting scream, she went over the side.

Dan scrambled up, feeling his heart leap and threaten to jump out of his chest.

'It's OK, Dan. She fell in the dinghy,' James called up. Panting, Dan leaned over the side and groaned at the sight of Cara, sprawled flat on her back with her eyes closed, on the bottom of the dinghy.

Wayne held up the metal box that was the emergency pack. 'Unfortunately, when she fell in, she hit her head on this.'

'Oh, oh.'

chapter eleven

I'm dead, Cara thought. *I'm dead and in Heaven, only…I never would have thought that you could have a splitting headache in Heaven. Or flies buzzing about. How am I supposed to enjoy Heaven if I have a big headache and I have to swat flies?*

'Cara, can you hear me?'

Oh, no. Now somebody was calling her. Didn't they know where she was? Wasn't there supposed to be some sort of bright light she could follow to the arrival lounge? Who was responsible for this mess-up?

'Cara, open your eyes.'

Eyes. Apparently, she still had eyes. All she had to do was lift her eyelids, but the effort was equal to trying to lift an anvil with an elephant sitting on top of it.

After one last momentous effort, Cara opened her eyes, and realised she wasn't in Heaven. She knew it wasn't Heaven because the concerned face looming above her was Dan's, and she was sure Dan must already have reservations in The Other Place.

'Wh-where am I?' she said, and winced both from the pain in her head and the cliché she'd just uttered.

'We're on Cobaar Island. Don't you remember?'

There was something to remember. With a bit of effort she might be able to wade through the cotton wool her head was stuffed with and come up with the necessary information. Mm…Cobaar Island. Yes. They were supposed to have gone there after Peter's boat started taking in water. Mum and Dad's dinghy had been full, and she had planned to hold on to the side, but Dan and

Peter had tried to stop her, and…that's all she could remember.

'What happened?'

'Other than you taking a leap like a member of The Flying Fruit-fly Circus and hitting your head on the way down? Nothing much. A storm, a rescue.'

'What?' Cara sat bolt upright and immediately regretted it. Pain lanced through her head once more, and her panties rode up her bottom. She groaned and lay back again, concentrating on the puffy white clouds floating above, which could quite reasonably have been carousing stars or twittering birds.

'Take it easy,' Dan said, smoothing her hair back from her forehead with one big warm hand. 'No serious damage done, but you can't just leap back into the land of the living that abruptly. Now, be a good girl and do as I say.'

'Don't tell me what to do. You're a comedian, not a doctor.'

'Well, actually…'

'Please, Dan, just tell me what happened, will you?'

'If you'll just let me speak! Like I said, you hit your head on the way down and were out cold. I pulled you out of the drink and into the dinghy and, soon after that, a storm whipped up.'

'A storm? But it was a beautiful day!'

Dan sighed impatiently. 'Don't you know anything, Cara? Even if you hadn't lived near the sea all your life, aren't there are enough literary clichés and real-life stories about the sea's moodiness to remind you that it's normal for it to go from calm to wild in a matter of minutes?'

'Of course I know!' she exclaimed, despite the pain that the higher decibels caused, annoyed that she'd been caught out. 'Where's everyone else?'

'Well, you know the rescue I just mentioned? Obviously it wasn't us.'

'Obviously. And given the usual turn of events when I'm with you, I'm not surprised. God, what a mess.'

Dan's face clouded over. 'You know, for a journalist, you certainly have an overactive imagination. I mean, are you actually going to write in your article that I'm a jinx? And which source are you going to quote? The X-files?'

Cara opened her mouth, but no words came. For once in her adult life, she had to admit he was totally right. Making him responsible for the raw prawn fiasco and her immature eavesdropping, claiming he was a jinx…it was behaviour that would have put the most temperamental adolescent to shame. And what was her defence? *He made me do it, Miss.*

Excuses. And weren't excuses the most convenient thing on the face of the earth? Because just before then, she had been face-to-face with the truth – she wanted Dan. She wanted him so badly that, yes, just like that crazy voice in her head suggested, she didn't think she could live without having him. And that kind of raw emotion, that handing over of sense and sensibility to someone else to run with, as if romance were some kind of demented rugby game, scared the life out of her. Robert had been safe. Blaming Dan for anything and everything was also safe. Anything, as a matter of fact, that made her look outwards to the world, or upwards to her head, instead of inwards to her heart, was safe. She had no idea why she did this, but the truth left a bad taste in her mouth. Still, being concussed on a desert island beach was no time for self-analysis, so she opted for the oldest, most trusted strategy for when you've been caught out. She changed the subject.

'So,' Cara tried to look nonchalant and in control, even

though guilt was prodding her that she should be apologising to Dan instead. 'What do we do now?'

'We wait.'

'Wait? Don't you remember anything from your scouting days? There's stuff to do! We need to build a shelter and find potable water, and build a signal fire…'

'As a matter of fact, if you didn't keep interrupting, you would have found out that I've already found shelter and we're got water purifying tablets, as well as flares, so we don't need to build a fire. And please, whatever you do, don't go to the bother of thanking me for actually saving your life or anything crass like that…'

He kept on ranting, but his voice suddenly became muffled as in the insulated chamber of her mind, guilt stopped prodding and drove one clear stab right through her chest. She was a bad, bad person. She had no shame. She would blame Dan for everything, even when he had *saved her life*. She could have drowned! Become shark bait! He could have let her drown and, after the way she had behaved, who would have blamed him?

For all his ranting and raving and rolling his eyes like a madman, she had to admit he really was lovely. He was a hero and he had saved her life and today his eyes had taken on the hue of the sky behind him, and he was lovely, really lovely. Unexpectedly cute for losing his patience with her now, too, even though these past few days he'd certainly had the right to lose it, but hadn't, which was lovely. Oh, he'd acted hurt and sullen a couple of times, but that had been it really and, even now, with all his going on and on and on, he was still rhythmically and very soothingly stroking her hair, and that was lovely.

'Dan…?'

He didn't hear, just kept on ranting, and instead of getting angry with him because of it, Cara was amused to find it rather cute. But he would have to be quiet, because there was something she needed to say, and she knew there was one sure way to shut him up.

Lifting her arm took a little less effort than opening her eyes had. Putting her hand behind Dan's neck took even less effort than lifting her arm. Pulling his head down towards her took a fraction of the effort of that. And kissing him gently but very soundly took no effort at all. When the kiss was finished, his diatribe didn't continue. All she heard were deep breaths as he rested his forehead on hers.

'I'm sorry,' she said softly. 'I'm sorry for everything. And thank you for saving my life.'

'You're welcome.'

'Please, Dan, can we start from the beginning? Tell me everything that happened, and I promise I'll listen.'

Dan did continue with the story and with the stroking of her hair, except that now he was very very close, and his breath was her breath, and his fingertips were straying from her hair to her cheeks and chin and throat and mouth. Now that she knew everyone was safe, his every touch was rearranging her priorities, so that suddenly what had happened didn't seem very important. But she had promised to listen, so she did.

'The storm whipped up, and our dinghies got separated. We just drifted further and further apart. By the time Ocean Rescue had airlifted the others, we were out of sight behind the bluff. Then it got dark and they stopped looking, I suppose.'

'So you mean I've been out like a light overnight?'

'Er – yeah. But you're OK, right?'

'Mm, yes. Actually,' she moved her body to further accommodate Dan on top and felt her skin react to his firm warmth, 'I feel surprisingly good.'

'That's good.' He smiled reassuringly and looked up

at the sky, and Cara noticed that not only was he close enough for her to hear his breathing, but also his heart-beat above the roar of the waves, and the vibrato calls of the silver gulls. 'All we've got to do is sit tight until they come to pick us up.'

'Sit tight? That's a diplomatic expression, isn't it? Here I was thinking we were stranded.'

He shrugged. 'Yeah, I suppose. But at least we're safe, aren't we?'

'Yes, but for how long?'

'Well, this looks like a good place to me. We're both OK, we've got our brains, and look...' He reached behind her and grabbed a metal box. 'An emergency pack. I think we can tough it out until the cavalry comes.'

'That's not quite what I meant,' Cara grinned. 'I mean, how long before we actually murder each other? We don't exactly get along at the best of times, do we? So – without society to keep us from getting at each other, how long do you think before the situation develops into "Lady of the Flies"?'

Dan laughed, then was serious. Very serious. 'Oh, I think society has kept us from each other long enough.' He traced her lips with a thumb, leaving a wake of delicious tingles. 'You're absolutely right, Cara. It's just you and me here, and there's nothing stopping us from doing what we really, really want to do. But you know, something tells me it involves the total opposite of killing each other.'

He was right. Society had indeed kept them from each other, but only because she'd let it. Cara St John, always looking upwards to the thoughts society had helped form in her head, looking outwards to what the world would think, and never looking within. The last time she had looked within, before she had let that stupid raw prawn incident muddy her vision, what had she seen? A want so big and deep and wide that it made the Grand Canyon look like a ditch. A want that she would have to fall, and fall, and fall into. Already she could feel the thrill of the fall, pumping adrenaline through her, readying her for the painful, agonising, exquisitely delicious bruises that would brand her Dan's, forever and ever. Because she had never wanted anyone as much as she wanted Dan, and would never want anyone like this again.

'And what, exactly,' she breathed, even though his face was now moving even closer and she knew she couldn't stop the fall even if she wanted to, 'is the opposite of killing each other?'

'This.'

He kissed her, and Cara felt him claim each and every one of her senses, including some she didn't even know she had, like the sense of *rightness*. It felt right. His kiss told her as much about herself as it did about him and, right now, it showed that there was a part of her that was either hidden or unused for far too long. A part of her that she and Dan could explore together. His kisses were for a totally different Cara, a Cara who only made an appearance for him, kissing him back expertly because, strangely enough, she wasn't an expert at kissing, but she was an expert at kissing Dan, bringing a stormy intensity into his eyes that didn't exist at any other time. A Cara who didn't feel the wash of ever-increasing tingles all over her body, from the soles of her feet to her very hair follicles, at any other time save with Dan. It was all about rediscovery, she supposed, but the important thing was that she couldn't rediscover this part of herself without rediscovering Dan. The two were inextricably linked.

As much as she wanted it, it frightened the hell out of her.

For whatever she discovered, there was absolutely no

future for them. Even if this wasn't Dan's ego trying to seduce her, there was no amount of attraction, or feeling of rightness, or lust or, yes, even love, that could survive the stress of trying to jam together two mismatched pieces of a puzzle.

Delicious as his kiss was, she pulled away. He went to speak, but she silenced him with a finger on his lips.

'Don't. Please, Dan, don't say anything,' she said softly. 'I know we want each other…'

'It's more than that!'

She shook her head, her heart inexplicably breaking for something she hadn't had, and yet had already lost. 'Whatever it is, this isn't a romance novel, Dan. We're too different! I mean, after the attraction, what's going to keep us together out of bed?'

'Different? Have you forgotten? We once said we were soul-mates, Cara.'

'Maybe we used to be…'

'You don't just stop being someone's soul mate! You either are, or are not.'

'Then we probably were never soul mates in the first place. We were…close. We were close, and we grew apart.'

'Then let's grow together again.'

Dan brought his lips to hers once more and, miraculously, Cara's internal argument just stopped. Afterwards, she had no idea what stopped it, but now she was only aware of him and of her, her mind totally engaged in the moment, perfectly echoing her body's awakening. She never would have suspected that she had a sexual organ inside her head, but now she knew.

His deepening kiss brought surrender, and with the surrender came power. Cara felt it take hold of her, so strong she could have screamed, but screaming wasn't what this was all about. The power had to have an outlet, and Dan was it.

She pushed against him and rolled him on to his back and, astride him, was able to feel his very own awakening as she kissed his gorgeous mouth, and chin, and neck, and then backtracked up to his ears. He moaned and shuddered, and Cara looked into his eyes and smiled, a smile of complete understanding and intimacy. He was beautiful, and he was hers for now, and nothing else mattered. Bit by bit, she divested him of every scrap of clothing, and then there he was, like a beached merman, golden skin and golden hair on golden sand, a magnificent sight that not only turned her on but made her feel privileged. She had imagined him like this before, and had thought that the only thing that should drape his body was her own. So, now that one half of her fantasy was complete, she could fulfil the other.

Cara stood before Dan, and he enjoyed her with his eyes as she took off her sandals and sundress. His wordless gasp as she took off her bra and panties did more for her libido than an entire lexicon of dirty words could have ever done. It took supreme control to take the time to remove the elastics and pins from her hair, and fluff it out to a mane that tumbled down her back and over her breasts.

'Cara, you are a goddess.'

'You make me feel like one.'

She knelt beside Dan, the hunger she felt for him gnawing at her from the inside out. She wanted him. She wanted to be joined to him from tangled hair to entwined toes, but first, she needed to get to know every square millimetre of him. She'd been deprived – he had been away so long, and instead of running from him these past few days, she could have been learning to love his quirky mind and his beautiful body... There was a lot of catching up to do.

And catch up she did, getting to know the look and feel and taste and smell of every part of him. The sound of him too, because for all her explorations, he was making noises she didn't know a man could make. When they were both so engorged in desire that bursting seemed a definite possibility, Cara threw one leg over his hips.

'Wait,' he managed to say. 'I know we're stranded on a desert island and everything, but I do happen to have some condoms…'

'Well, what do you know?' she grinned. 'You are a big – a very big – Boy Scout after all.'

'Mind you,' he breathed as he finished putting one on and swung Cara astride him again, 'later on, when this is over, we'll have to do something about the sand rash and the sunburn…'

Both cried out at the moment of bonding. The combined pain and pleasure on both her body and soul at the birth of the third entity – the *we* – that their union created was so intense that she had to clench her eyes shut, willing herself inwards to remain contained. Dan raised himself up and placed his arms around her.

'It's good, it's fine,' he whispered. 'Don't go anywhere, my love. Stay with me…'

Forcing herself from her inward retreat was a momentous act of courage and trust. It meant giving herself completely to Dan, no holds barred – body, mind, and soul. An exposé that would make even the most low-down tabloid seem like a high school yearbook. She had hidden herself from Dan for so long – did she dare let him tap into the well of her essence? Was she ready to accept what both of them might find?

The questions were frightening, but the answer was an exhilarating 'yes'.

She opened her eyes and found herself face-to-face with truth. With love. Pure unadulterated love in Dan's deep blue eyes and, she realised, love surging through her. The real Cara, the real Dan, communicating at long last, not just through their bodies but through the quintessential connection of their eyes. Her entire being sang, 'I love him!' and the joy that burbled up made her laugh out loud. She never would have imagined anyone laughing during lovemaking, but there was no other outlet for it. She felt like a magnifying glass, and joy was streaming through her like sunlight. Dan, basking in it, smiled.

Here they both were, as they were obviously meant to be. They had travelled different roads to get there, but it didn't matter. What mattered was that they were there now and that they should go on together. And Cara had an initial destination in mind. She pushed Dan back on to the sand, and mentally kissed the skin on her knees goodbye.

'Isn't it funny,' Cara said, several lovemaking sessions later, as Dan dabbed Betadine from the emergency pack on their knees and elbows, 'how I said I wouldn't have anything to do with you if we were stuck on a desert island with wild pigs for company? And here we are. Is this a great cosmic joke, or what?'

Dan looked up from blowing on her stinging knee and smiled, then froze. 'Goats. Wild goats.'

'No, Dan, I distinctly remember saying "wild pigs". I said wild pigs because...'

'No,' Dan swallowed and kept looking at some point behind her, 'I mean wild goats. Here. Now.'

Cara felt the hairs on the back of her neck stand up and, although she really, really didn't want to, she turned around. Pawing at the ground between the clumps of tea-tree was a very large goat with very big horns, and a very bad attitude.

'What the…'

'Run!'

Quicker than a jack-in-the-box on his fourth cup of coffee, Dan sprang to his feet, grabbed Cara's hand and yanked her up. Cara thought that not since the violins in the 'Psycho' shower scene had she heard a more frightening sound than the goat's bleating as he charged. She had no idea what they had done to annoy this cross-looking goat, but stopping to think about it was not a good idea. She ran. And screamed. She kept right on screaming as she followed Dan into the bush and then up the nearest tree, which, amazingly, had no hand or footholds, she could see. They did so just in time to hear a sickening *thunk* against the trunk of the tree, which shuddered against the impact.

Holding on to their respective branches, Cara and Dan looked down. The goat had its head down, ready for another blow.

Thunk!

'Jeez!' Dan exclaimed.

'Umm…Dan? Is there anything you can do to make it go away?'

Dan leaned down and tried to catch the goat's eye. 'Hey, goat! Shoo!'

Thunk!

Dan sighed and straightened himself up. 'Ah, well. We'll just have to wait it out. I mean, he'll get tired of this eventually.'

'When exactly did you say the goat will get tired of this?' Cara asked, half-an-hour later.

'Eventually.'

Thunk!

'Oh.' Cara bit her lip. 'Isn't there anything else you can throw down to him?'

Dan had been holding the emergency pack when they started running and, unbelievably, had managed to hold it, run and climb at the same time. A triumph of the human spirit!

'Uh-uh. I've already thrown down all the food bars and the chocolate *and* their wrappers. Unless you think he'd like to eat sunscreen or water purifying tablets, there's nothing else.'

'I see.'

'Still, it's a nice day for it, don't you think?'

Thunk!

Cara sighed, but had to smile up at him. Even though they were stranded on a desert island with no food and a homicidal goat trying to ram their tree down, there was nowhere else she would have rather been.

'Dan?'

'Hmm?'

'That part in your first movie, where you stomped on the girl's dress because she had paint all over it…that wasn't what happened to us that night, was it?'

He shrugged and nodded. 'Yep. I'm afraid it was.'

'And to think I've been holding it against you all these years.'

Thunk!

'Ah well,' Dan sighed. 'It wasn't surprising, really. You had no reason to listen to me, not after all those years of merciless teasing.'

There was a brief silence – not taking into account, of course, the goat's head ramming against the trunk of the tree.

'Dan?'

'Hmm?'

'Why did you do it? All the teasing, I mean?'

'Well, you know adolescent boys, always teasing the girl they like best.'

'Yeah, that's what Pia says. I don't buy it.'

Thunk!

'That's what it was, at least in the beginning.' Dan gave her a crooked smile. 'We'd been best friends, and then you began to change, way before I did. You in your training bra and crush on John Travolta – I just couldn't relate! At least when we were at each other, we had something in common. But then, it became a whole new ball-game.' He looked up at the sky, as if he could find the appropriate words spelled out in the clouds. 'You really did get serious and uptight. That wasn't my Cara, and I was going to shake you out of it, no matter what! I just couldn't stand back and let them do it to you...'

'"Them"? You weren't going to let who do what to me?'

Dan shrugged. 'School. The system. You know.'

'No, I don't.'

'You don't remember?'

'No!'

Thunk!

'Stupid goat. Look, we can't continue a conversation like this...'

'Yes, we can! Now tell me, Dan!'

Dan looked at her long and hard, then sighed in resignation. 'OK, just so long as you're not expecting the meaning of life or anything. They were little things, I suppose, but the sort of little thing that makes a difference when you're a kid.' He paused. 'Do you remember in Year Seven, how angry you were when you had to do that talk in class about your chosen profession?'

Cara tried to remember but couldn't. She shook her head.

'You were in Ray Coulter's class at the time, and he got each one of you to stand up and say what you were

going to be when you grew up. You said you were going
to be what you were right now – a writer. He just said,
"How can you call yourself a writer? To be a writer, you
must have travelled, you must have lived!" You came
home ranting and raving about it, saying they were
typical words from someone who'd never written a word
in his life. Pat told Mum what happened, and I heard all
about it afterwards.'

'What a horrible thing to say to a child! How can
anyone with a conscience put a damper on kids' dreams
like that?' It occurred to Cara that it also explained her
'if you write, you're already a writer' speech to Marie.

Thunk!

'Unfortunately, I can tell you from experience, that it
was typical of the attitude of much of Toongalla High at
the time. They were good at the lip service, you know?
"You can do it, blah blah blah, follow your dreams, blah
blah blah", but they never followed through. When I said
I wanted to be a comedian, my teacher laughed! But
when she saw I actually meant it, she told me to get my
studies out of the way first. The *right* studies of course
– Heaven forbid she suggest performance arts or writing!
It had to be something "to fall back on if you fail".' He
rolled his eyes. 'That "if" really gets to me. It might as
well be a "when".'

'Yeah, I know what you mean. So did you?'

'Did I, what?'

'Get the right sort of degree.'

Dan cleared his throat. 'Umm…yes I did, but only
because I wanted to, not as a backup or anything.
Anyway – back to you. I remember you'd been
changing, growing up, I suppose, but the biggest change
came after the Career Fair.'

'I remember Career Day!' Cara smiled.

'Do you remember what happened?'

'Hmm – yeah,' she nodded. 'It was a huge thing, it took up the entire hall. There were representatives from colleges and universities and industry, and parents came and spoke about their jobs. Dad came and spoke.'

Dan looked at her intently. 'No, that's the whole point. He didn't.'

'What?' she frowned.

'You told Ray Coulter that your Dad would be happy to speak at the fair and he refused. He said that having your Dad there would give the Toongalla High kids unrealistic expectations. That they needed to hear from people established in *real* jobs.' Cara said nothing, but her eyes filled with tears. 'I think that's when you decided you were going to be a journalist, instead of a writer.'

Cara blinked a few times, wiping the tears back to where they came from. She remembered now. She remembered the hurt, dismay, and embarrassment – for both herself and her father. But it would never have happened if Dad had just decided to stick to journalism.

'You know, Dan, I don't understand.' She shook her head. 'Dad's never regained the respect he had when he was a journalist. I know he started writing kids' books to make ends meet, but why didn't he just give it up when he'd put me through school? I mean, it wasn't like he was hard up for money or anything...'

'Cara, I think you've got it all wrong. Your dad told us that he always wanted to write for children – but his father insisted he learn a trade instead. Journalism, "just to fall back on". Sound familiar? So it wasn't that he wrote kids' books to make ends meet; he actually *worked as a journalist* to make ends meet. He was a journalist only until he got himself established as a fiction writer.' Dan reached over and put his hand on Cara's cheek. 'This is all stuff you could have found out for yourself a long time ago if you had taken the time to just sit down and talk – I mean really talk – with your dad.'

Thunk!

Dan looked down and shook his head. 'This goat just isn't going to let up. Listen – I'll lead him away from here and you get back to camp. It'll be dark in a couple of hours.'

'Will you be OK?'

'Are you kidding?' He gave his best movie star's smile. 'I'm "Mikhail McHale", remember?'

With a kiss and a smile, Dan lowered himself by his arms, sinews extending and then releasing as he made the final leap down to land. He hit the ground running, which was just as well because the goat was on his case. With a caveman yell, Dan took off through the bush, the goat following close behind.

Cara let herself down from the tree cautiously and began the walk back to their camp on the beach.

Facts, she thought, *had once been my friends. Now I have to exchange facts for something more profound... truth.*

The facts remained the same, but the truth they contained was now completely different. The truth was, she seemed to have spent a lifetime making Dan responsible for something which was far larger than the result of mere teasing.

She realised now that she was the product of a particular culture – a culture which she resented, but still desperately wanted to please. She had exchanged her dreams for Toongalla's expectations, and yet hated going back there. It wasn't surprising. Subconsciously, Toongalla was the site of a lost battle. And Dan? Darling Dan, he had never done anything seriously wrong. So why had she spent so much time and energy avoiding him? Perhaps she also resented the fact that he'd done what she, herself, had clearly failed to do – he had gone out in the world to fulfil his dreams.

Yes, but did it make a difference as to why she had become a journalist? Did it make a difference why she took herself so seriously? Did it make a difference why she felt the way she did about her dad? This last pill was the one that stuck in her throat. Now, as an adult, she should be indignant at what Ray Coulter had said about her dad, but she couldn't be. That would have been the pot calling the kettle black…and a whole lot of other clichés about hypocrisy. At the end of the day, what Ray Coulter thought about James St John didn't matter. But what James St John's daughter thought about him was another thing entirely.

Sure, she loved her dad, but she didn't respect him. And was love without respect really love at all? If it was, then it most certainly was a Clayton's love – the love you have when you don't want to put much effort into a relationship. She saw that her issues with respect had somehow coloured almost every relationship she'd ever had. She had bestowed respect like a knighthood, judging who deserved it and who didn't, and never stopping to analyse what she respected in the first place. She had respected Robert…Robert, for Heaven's sakes! A person whose entire existence was based on the belief that he was superior to everyone else. What about her dad? Dan? Surely they were worthy of her respect too?

With sudden clarity, Cara realised that this was what her relationship with Robert had been all about. Keeping love and respect totally separate from each other, treating them as issues that never mixed. Robert had been convenient, because the very things which she had wanted in her life, were the things which she herself did not respect. She had wanted the kids, the romance, the domestic bliss with its harmonious blend of the mundane and the heavenly; the evenings spent writing and creating worlds of make-believe. She had wanted it all – and had been frightened to death of achieving it. She could never respect herself for wanting such things, and being with Robert had ensured she didn't get them.

Cara sighed painfully. Admitting a lifetime's folly wasn't easy – but strangely enough, she felt refreshed. As if someone had opened the window into her very soul and a cleansing breeze was now flowing through her.

Cara stepped out on to the warm sand, sand so golden pure that it was literally squeaky clean. Shading her eyes against the raw-red sun, she looked out across the clear water and saw, dimly in the distance, the mainland. The visual connection was comforting, but this island might as well have been a different world. Instead of the roar of traffic, she had the roar of surf. Instead of human voices, she could hear the cackle and chatter of birds. Instead of the Gold Coast's high-rise buildings, the tall slim cypress trees pointed up to the sky. The wind caressed her skin, whispering softly in her ears. Beyond the peace and quiet of a lonely place, this was the peace of insight, the peace of healing.

She heard a 'Cooee!' and, looking up the beach, she saw Dan running towards her, no goat in sight.

She smiled and waved.

Things were going to be different when she got back to the mainland. She didn't know how, but it would be a wonderful journey finding out.

'Look what I found.'

Cara turned at the sound of Dan's voice and found herself face-to-face with an armoured insect-like creature. She screamed.

'What on earth is it?'

'Moreton Bay bug. We are just out of Moreton Bay, you know. Let's build a fire and have ourselves a nice little feast.'

'But – it's alive!'

Dan looked askance at her. 'The ones you eat in restaurants were alive once too. Did you think they grew on trees or something?'

Cara threw up her hands and turned her back on him. 'OK, OK. I'll eat them, but I'm not cooking them, and I'm definitely not watching you cook them.'

Dan chuckled and set about rekindling last night's fire. Thankfully the emergency pack was well stocked, and had also included a billycan, mess kits, and wind- and waterproof matches. She sat on the sand and watched Dan, enjoying the absorbed, happy look on his face as he built up the fire with crisp seaweed and twigs, whistling to himself as he worked. It dawned on her that she had been smiling all the time she had been watching him. She loved Dan. It was soppy, but she could now see she had always loved him, and would always love him. But what of the future?

Things were going to be different, she knew, but Dan's life was still like nothing she could imagine sharing with him. She didn't know what lay ahead, but she was certain it didn't include living in reality-starved Los Angeles, or kissing the air beside the cheeks of the beautiful and the famous, or being the latest one in the tabloids' line of fire. Something hot and painful ignited in the pit of her stomach, as she envisioned the possibility of a life without Dan. While she had kept Dan at arm's length she had been relatively safe – despite the changes he'd wrought. But now that she had given herself to him, and opened herself to the wondrous gifts he had to offer, he was more precious than ever. Unbearable to let go. Now that she had tasted the sweetness of being one with Dan, how could she ever go back to being one on her own?

This morning, she had received the most amazing gift life had yet offered her – waking up in Dan's arms. His warmth and musky, sun-kissed scent had been the first thing she had been aware of, and his voice the first sound she heard, as with his face buried in her hair he murmured, 'Cara, my darling. I love you.' That moment had been worth a lifetime's wait, the fulfilment eclipsing any recognition she had received from her career or Robert, or anything else. This morning, however, would also most certainly bring rescue.

Back to the real world.

Cara could not see beyond this deserted island and the now. *Maybe that's the way it's supposed to be*, she thought. *Maybe I'm just supposed to savour the moment, and when the time comes to kiss him goodbye, I must do it without regrets.* These few days with Dan had already changed her forever, and that in itself was an enormous gift. Maybe it was too much to expect to find a happy-ever-after middle ground where they could both meet. What was it that people said? That you can never marry your first love? Although losing the one you love is like losing a limb, people said you manage to go on. She couldn't see how, but apparently it was possible.

She hadn't bitten her nails for many years, but she began biting them again now. She welcomed the pain as she drew blood, as if it could even begin to deflect the hurt she felt inside.

'Ready for breakfast?' Dan called over his shoulder.

Cara forced a smile. *Enjoy the moment*, she said to herself. 'Are you kidding? After the one barley sugar for dinner last night?'

'Lucky the goat didn't eat those as well. Tuck in.'

Dan and Cara busied themselves cracking the hot

shells of the Moreton Bay bugs with their bare hands, extracting the sweet flesh from them and popping them into their mouths with contented sighs. She'd had Moreton Bay bugs – called bugs for their appearance, even though they were crustaceans – before in restaurants, served in all sorts of sophisticated and rich concoctions, but never had they tasted as delicious as this. She looked across at Dan, relishing every bite, and knew that it was because of this beautiful man, who had fed her both body and soul.

'Dessert?' she smiled and, standing up, she took off her sundress.

chapter twelve

Much later, Dan lay sated and asleep beside Cara on the sand, sighing in his dreams, the warmth from his naked body seeping into her skin and through to her very bones. She smoothed the hair back from his face and kissed his forehead.

'I love you,' she whispered. It seemed simpler to say it when he was asleep.

Cara knew Dan loved her. After what they had shared here, she knew it had been stupid to believe he had merely wanted to bed her. But still, admitting to loving him while he was awake would be complicating things. Her heart hammered at the thought that soon they would be separated, and she stood up. A walk would calm her down.

She put on her dress and shoes, wrote 'Gone Exploring' on the sand at his feet, and set out through the spinifex, then bush, and the line of cypress.

It was a beautiful day but still no sign of Ocean Rescue. She laughed to herself. Although realistically she knew they had to go back, it was fun to fantasise about what would happen if they didn't. If they were to stay here, there'd be no dilemma. Just Dan and Cara on a beautiful island paradise. They could have lots of babies and a tree house just like the Swiss Family Robinson.

Or, instead of the tree house, a luxurious, whitewashed villa with a jetty, a swimming pool, and a tennis court.

Just like the one she could see right now!

About 100 metres ahead.

Cara broke into a run. This wasn't a desert island after all! They were saved! The idea of her and Dan peacefully living on an island forever was as unrealistic as living together out of it, so being rescued took sudden, top-most priority. She ran up the paved driveway, through the formally landscaped garden, and panting, pounded on the door.

'Hello? Hello! Please help!'

After several tries, she got no answer, and could have wept with frustration. There was nothing for it but to try the door handle. This was something she never would have done in ordinary circumstances, but desperate times called for desperate measures. She laughed out loud when the door actually opened under her cautious pushing.

'Anybody home?' she called as she poked her head through the door.

There was no answer and so she let herself into the most luxurious domestic foyer she had ever seen in her life. The marble floor made her footsteps echo up to the high atrium ceilings, but the sound was then absorbed by the bubbling of a fountain set among the ferns that luxuriated under an enormous skylight.

Again she called out, but all was quiet, and her journalist's curiosity took over. The first door she came to led to a sitting room – although she couldn't imagine anyone sitting there because they actually wanted to. It was one of those clinical, stark white rooms with designer chairs, which were only comfortable for humans with no buttocks.

However, there was a door in the far corner, and Cara went through it into an infinitely more comfortable entertainment area, with enormous puffy chairs set in front of a panoramic television screen, and the mother of all stereo systems. One wall was reinforced with a row of old-fashioned pinball machines, and another was covered with photographs.

Most of the photographs featured a man who looked extremely familiar to Cara. When she saw several of him in what appeared to be movie sets, he immediately snapped into context. He was an actor – one of those character actors whom you see constantly, but never quite remember their name – mostly because they've never had any starring roles.

This particular actor – whatever his name was – had worked constantly for over thirty years in television and movies, all over the English-speaking world. He had one of those nondescript faces that, combined with his acting skills, could make him look royal or destitute, benign or dastardly, attractive or repulsive, according to what the role demanded.

Cara smiled as she recognised familiar movie stills…before she suddenly became very still herself. There was a shot of the actor with Dan on the 'Mikhail McHale' set. Of course! He had played the part of Herr X's unfortunate accountant. Which on its own meant nothing much, except that right next to *that* picture… there was another one.

A picture of the actor standing proudly next to his car.

Not just any car, but a Morgan Three-wheeler.

A Morgan Three-wheeler just like the one which she had hit.

In fact…*it was the very same one!*

Her mind snapped into gear as she now recognised the man who'd demanded that she pay up…it was *this* actor. Except, of course, that he'd been wearing glasses, a false moustache and thick wig eyebrows at the time.

She also immediately realised that the so-called 'accident' had been a complete set-up.

And could it be…that if that had been a set-up, then

the two of them being stranded on Cobaar Island was a set-up too? What was it that Anna had laughingly said to her? 'Stay away from those raw prawns?'

Her heart hammered as she began to pace, then walk. What had Dan done? She had never experienced anything as intensely real as she and Dan had shared on Cobaar Island. So real, that her life up until that point had seemed a lie. And yet...if her suspicions were correct and Dan had set this all up, everything that had happened here had to be a lie as well!

Proof. She needed proof. She didn't want it, but she needed it. There they were, those conflicting needs and wants again. She didn't want to believe that Dan had done this thing, but she needed to know. If ever she wanted to find her bearings again, and make some sense of the emotional turbo churning up her insides, she needed to know the truth.

Cara took a deep breath and steeled herself as she paced through the beautiful house, but it revealed no further clues. As she walked out of the house, however, her ears registered something faint but distinct. Voices and music. Coming from the boat shed.

Quietly but swiftly she sneaked down to the boat shed. Ignoring a thought that she should at least pause and listen through the door, she heaved the door open, only barely restraining an impulse to kick it open and yell, 'Freeze!'

As it was, she didn't have to shout for anyone to freeze because they did it all on their own. There were Peter and Scott, one moment playing cards and quaffing beer, and the next moment not. The only mobile thing was Peter's cigarette tilting downwards and then falling as if in slow motion from his mouth on to the table.

She crossed her arms and gave Peter and Scott a savage look. The fresh sweat beaded on their upper lips, and their bobbing Adam's apples as they gulped, told her she was looking and acting formidable enough to warrant some long-overdue respect.

'Hello, boys. So nice of you to come and rescue us in our hour of need. Were you actually planning on letting us know you were here, or did Dan already know?'

Her words broke the spell and set the men in motion. They sprang upright with a scraping of chairs, coughing and spluttering.

'Cara! Where…what are you…?'

'What a relief! We've been out of our minds…'

Cara rolled her eyes. 'Oh, cut it out, guys. The deal is spill, and spill quickly, before your photos appear front page centre in the loudest, garish tabloid with the headline, "Perverted Playboys in Passionate Pleasure Paradise".'

And spill quickly they did.

Heavens above, how could she have been so stupid? Cara berated herself as they told her the whole story. Right from the beginning, Dan had orchestrated them being together for the week. Hutch had been in cahoots all this time – it was the reason why he had inexplicably insisted that she was the only person for the job. When she had refused, Dan had organised for this actor – whatever his name was! – to get in her way so she could cause grievous bodily harm to his precious Morgan. And – oh no, she thought with fresh dismay – that must mean that Pia and Lucie had been in cahoots as well! Not only was it Pia who had convinced her to go for that drive, but it was Pia and Lucie who had left Dan alone in her flat to wreck her relationship with Robert.

But the crowning achievement had to be this bogus stranding. Anything could have happened! She'd seen 'The Blue Lagoon' when she was twelve, so she knew the score. But that was nothing. She had been unconscious for twenty four hours, with no medical attention. Did Dan have no conscience? As a matter of fact, did anyone else? All of them must have been in on it – Peter, Scott, Anna, and both sets of parents! Since Dan had arrived, there was no one – no friends, no family – she could trust, no one above his influence. Only one person…

An injection of adrenaline set Cara's heart racing with overwhelming fear.

Marie.

Jamie had said not to take too long in seeing Marie, and had suggested that even Sunday might be too long. It was now Tuesday! Cara bit her fist hard but was unable to stop the tears springing to her eyes.

Always joking, always playing, aren't you Dan? Well, you can't play with people's hearts.

This was too much. His arrogance in believing that her life could be dismantled and rebuilt into something of his own design was inexcusable. Like a Robert with a hyperactive imagination. She had given herself to Dan, heart and soul, and would now without a doubt suffer for it. He had also kept her away from Marie and – she shivered at the thought – there was a good chance she would suffer for that too. But, far more importantly, he had stopped Cara from doing something that would make a real difference in a life that could quite possibly soon be over.

The combination of hurt and anger was a potent cocktail, and she drank deep. *Oh no, Dan Hunter, you won't keep this time*, she vowed. Vengeance would be swift and immediate.

'Get the boat ready,' Cara said to Peter and Scott, her face set in stone, anaesthetising her heart in preparation for what was about to happen. 'I'll be back in a few minutes.'

With quick strides, she made her way back to the house, picked up the phone, and dialled the Channel 11 number.

'Hello? Newsroom, please.' She paused as she was connected through. 'Good morning, this is Cara St John from the *Clarion*. May I speak to Heather Sumner, please?'

'Yes?' Heather's voice was like an Arctic blast down the phone line. Cara bit her lip to keep from smiling in wry amusement.

'Heather. Thank you for agreeing to speak to me. I called to apologise for my appalling behaviour the other night. It was immature and totally inexcusable.'

'Oh.' Heather's surprise was obvious. 'All right – apology accepted.'

'Thank you. You and Robert make a wonderful couple, and since I care about you both, I can only wish you the utmost happiness together.'

'Well…thank you! I'm so glad you see it that way.'

'Oh yes. You're perfect for each other. Now, will you let me make it up to you?'

'Really, Cara, there's no need…'

'Oh, yes there is. And you'll love this one, Heather. A Dan Hunter exclusive.'

Cara chuckled to herself as she hung up. *Let's see how Dan likes being on the receiving end of one of* my *jokes.*

Oh yeah, she thought a little while later as Peter sailed the 'Star of the Sea' out of the jetty. A journo's instinct is a thing of beauty. Fast and smooth, the yacht rounded the bluff to the beach where Dan still lay, naked and asleep on the sand. At that very same moment, all three heard the staccato thumping of the Channel 11 helicopter blades chopping the air.

Cara looked up and smiled, then turned to the two men innocently.

'A news helicopter! What a coincidence.' She took a loudhailer from the cabin and leaned over the side. 'Hey, Dan! Dan!' Cara saw him sit bolt upright then, face dawning in horror, stand up in all his buff glory. She pointed upwards to the helicopter now hovering above, a cameraman hanging out of the open door. 'Say cheese!'

'Not one word.' Cara cautioned as she swept past her gob-smacked mother into the house. Her father rushed out of his study and she pointed at him. 'Not one word from you either.'

'Cara, are you – are you all right?'

'Save it, Dad. I know exactly what happened, so don't embarrass yourself by pretending you think I'm return-ing from a watery grave.'

'But…'

Cara grasped his shoulders. 'No "buts". You and I need to talk. Dan did convince me of that – but not right now.' She turned to face her mother and gave her a look of warning. 'Dan did not, however, convince me of anything else, so don't get your hopes up. I'm having a shower and then I'm going back to Brisbane. Dad, please have the books for Marie ready by the time I'm set to leave.' She walked away, then stopped and came back. 'Mum, please ring the high school and tell Ray Coulter that I won't be there to give my speech today – and Dan probably won't be either.'

'But…' Pat shyly ventured, 'that's not until tomorrow.'

'What?' Cara narrowed her eyes. 'What day is it today?'

'Monday.'

Cara groaned. More lies! Dan had led her to believe she had been unconscious for twenty four hours but, given the time of day it had been when she had taken the flying leap, and then regained consciousness, it had

probably been just the few minutes it took to get to
Cobaar Island. Wayne would have checked her out to
make sure she was OK, and then racked off with
everyone else. How could there have been so much
destruction in such a short time?

Cara felt like a human whirlwind as she packed,
grabbed her father's books, and the keys to Pat's car
without asking or thanking. They owed her big.
Although she did not break the speed limit, even the
drive to Brisbane passed as in fast-forward. This
speeded-up sensation was a blessing, because she feared
that if she were to slow down to analyse her feelings,
she'd collapse into a quivering mass of nerves and
weeping, unable to function ever again.

She screeched into a parking bay at Brisbane Children's Hospital and bounded up the stairs two at a time,
not caring about working up a sweat in her best work
suit, or her red-faced panting once she made it to the
cancer ward.

But Marie's bed was empty.

The physical stop was also the stop of whatever it was
that had kept her going since discovering Dan's deceit.
A wave of despair and desolation swept over her so
quickly and completely that she was literally left gasping
for air, unable to see how she could possibly live another
agonising minute. But she had to move. With great
effort, she managed to get her feet moving, and she
slowly turned and shuffled her way to the nurses' station.
The first person she saw was Jamie, mopping at her eyes
with a damp tissue.

'Jamie?' she managed to croak. 'Is Marie…'

'Gone?' She nodded. 'Yes. We're going to miss her so
much.'

A gulping sob escaped Cara's lips and she put a hand
up to her mouth, as if containing the sound could

somehow contain her grief. 'When?'

'An hour ago.'

Cara slumped and dumped the pile of books on the counter. 'I'd brought her these...' she said stupidly.

Jamie sniffed and gave her a watery smile. 'That's wonderful. Look…' she glanced around to make sure no one was around and lowered her voice. 'I know it's against the rules but if you promise to keep quiet I'll give you her address. I'm sure Jeanette wouldn't mind – Jeanette is Marie's mum.'

Cara nodded and Jamie took a file from a pile on the desk. She opened it and placed it on the counter. 'Oh, look,' she said casually, 'someone's left Marie's file open on the counter. I'd better put it away – as soon as I come back from my tea break.'

With a wink, Jamie walked away and Cara quickly glanced at the file. There was her name, Marie Smith, and her address just below. Silently repeating the address to herself she walked away, wondering what she could possibly say to Marie's mother. From all that Marie had said, she sounded like an extraordinary woman, but she doubted that there was any amount of strength that could ever prepare a parent for the loss of a child.

The books were useless now, she supposed, but still she hugged them as she slowly walked up the path to Marie's house. What was she doing here? She hadn't been close to Marie and would probably just be intruding, but she hadn't been able to keep away. Through the fog of shock, Cara understood that her heart didn't just ache for this bright girl who had wanted to be a writer but had her life's promise taken from her. She also ached for the similar girl Cara had once been. Being here meant acknowledging both.

She paused briefly with her fist in the air, and then knocked. Far too soon, the door was flung open and she found herself facing a brightly smiling woman with close-cropped red hair and a nose ring, in a beaded Indian muslin dress.

'Jeanette Smith?'

'Yes?'

'Hi. I'm Cara St John. I…'

'Cara! I've heard all about you!' Jeanette extended a hand, and drew her in through the door into a warm peaceful place echoing with soft ambient music, and the many wind chimes hanging beside open windows. Cara breathed in a strangely comforting bouquet of burning incense and spicy cooking. 'Please come in. Marie! Guess who's here!' she called out.

Cara froze, unable to comprehend whether it was her or Jeanette who was going nuts.

Jeanette put a hand on Cara's arm, concern darkening her radiant features. 'Good Gopal, Cara, what's the matter? You look like you've seen a ghost!'

'Well,' Cara chuckled humourlessly, her lips dry, 'almost. See, at the hospital, they said Marie, was – you know – *gone*.'

Jeanette stared at her and blinked a few times. 'Oh!' she finally exclaimed. 'And you thought they meant…*gone*?' Cara could only nod, tell-tale tears once more pooling in her eyes. Jeanette threw her hands up and then embraced Cara, giving her a hard squeeze. 'You poor thing, I can see how upset you are. Believe me, I am overjoyed to say Marie is still very much here. She just discharged herself from the hospital.'

'But everyone said things weren't looking that good.'

'That's right, they aren't at the moment. Perhaps it would be better if you heard the story from Marie herself.'

Relief like cool water washed through Cara, and it was no effort to smile, even through the tears, as she stepped into the kitchen. Marie was sitting at the table, looking to the door expectantly. She still looked quite weak and pale, but there was no mistaking the happy look on her face.

'Carrot-top, you found me! And look – your hair is all out and curly!'

'Yes. My dad sent you something.'

She placed the books on Marie's lap and laughed at her delighted squeals and cries of 'Mum! Look!' Finally, she grabbed Cara by the shoulders and pulled her down, then gave her a resounding kiss on the cheek.

'Thanks, Cara. You'll stay for dinner, won't you?'

Cara smiled and shook her head. 'Oh, no, I couldn't…'

'Why not? You have to eat, don't you?'

'Yes, but…'

'Great! We'll set another place. Mum has made my favourite dinner. I'm going to find out if my taste buds didn't die from lack of use at the hospital! There's cashew nut curry, and dhal, and raita, and Mum even made some naan. Much better than vanilla ice cream and jelly.'

'All right, all right!' Cara laughed and threw her hands up. 'I surrender!'

It was a delicious meal and Cara felt so at home and among friends that over the peppermint tea and dried fruit, she leaned over and asked Marie, 'So – why did you discharge yourself out of hospital?'

'Because I've had enough,' Marie shrugged.

'Wh–what did the doctors say?'

'They said that my T-cells are down, and that I need another course of chemotherapy and radiotherapy. But I told them that I was going home.'

Cara was dismayed. She could not imagine the world without Marie's bright presence. And, despite the fact that they had only met twice, this girl had claimed a piece of her heart, and she had to admit to not being able to imagine her own life without her either. 'But…you can't just give up!'

Marie laughed. 'Me? Give up?' She shook her head. 'It's not giving up, it's just making a different choice. Cara, I've been fighting this since I was eight-years-old. I almost can't remember what it's like not to have constant tests, constant treatment. I've had enough.'

Jeanette looked across at Marie and smiled. 'We'll be trying alternative therapies next. Naturopaths, homeopaths, meditating, cleansing retreats – whatever it takes, just as long as it's not damaging to her soul.'

'Yes,' Marie nodded. 'I don't know when I will die, just like you don't know when you will. But I can tell you, the day I die, it will be after a lot of fun, a lot of writing, and a lot of Mum's food. And I will have a full head of hair, just like Fiamma. Or you.'

Cara gazed at mother and daughter, who were smiling in perfect understanding and purpose at each other, and then something within her let go in a great big rush. Suddenly her eyes and nose were streaming, and her heart was breaking.

'Cara, what's wrong?'

It took a few hiccups and abortive starts, but Marie and Jeanette waited patiently until Cara smiled through the tears and mucus, and took handfuls from the tissue box on the coffee table. 'Marie, you are the bravest and most clear-thinking person I've ever met. You put me to shame.'

'What are you talking about, Carrot-top?'

'I'm immature and I'm a big fat coward!' she wailed. Out came the story, all of it, from Dan and Cara promising to marry each other in the cubby house, to the bashed Morgan, to being stuck on a supposedly desert island being chased by wild goats.

'Oh-my-gosh! He actually set all of it up so he could be with you?' Marie swooned dramatically and laid her head on Jeanette's shoulder. 'That's the most romantic thing I've ever heard!'

'Yes, but...' Cara clenched her fists and shook them, 'It was all lies!'

'Oh, give me a break!' Marie exclaimed. 'The feelings weren't lies!'

'It doesn't matter – how could there be a future for us? Our lives are totally different! There's no middle ground where we can meet.'

Jeanette leaned over and put a hand on Cara's knee. 'Cara, I don't understand. If feelings don't matter, and you thought there was no future for you two even when you were on the island, why are you upset now? Other than having a day off work, nothing's changed. Surely you're no worse off than you were before?'

'Yes, I am!' Cara was emphatic, even though Jeanette's argument made sense. Except for one thing.

Jeanette had said 'nothing's changed'. That's where the theory collapsed, of course. For Cara, everything had changed. Her heart, her mind, her view of her world past, present and future – it was all different.

Slowly, as if emerging from a mist, her dilemma became clearer and clearer until she felt she could put it into words. 'It's...it's...what Dan showed me. That my life wasn't what I wanted. That I wasn't who I wanted to be. I can't go back to what I had before him. And yet – I can't have what I really want.' Feelings *did* matter. So very much. As did the hopeless hope that she and Dan could somehow be together. She looked from Jeanette to Marie searchingly. 'Where am I supposed to go from here?'

Jeanette smiled, an infinitely wise and warm smile

that somehow seeped into Cara's bones and gave her strength. 'Oh, I think in your heart you know exactly where you're supposed to go.'

'You're what!' Pia yelled.

'You heard,' Cara said, closing the door to the apartment behind her. 'I'm going home. To Toongalla. For an indefinite period.'

'But Cara – why?' Lucie searched her eyes for clues.

'I need to, that's why. Did you think the little plan you helped Dan out with would have no repercussions? Well, to cut a long story short, it did. You're looking at a woman on the edge, girls. I love him, and I love you two, but working out whether I jump or fall of the edge is nothing to do with anyone else but me.'

'Will you stop talking in riddles?' Pia threw her hands up in the air. 'What plan? What edge?'

Cara paused briefly to look at both of them, then smiled crookedly. 'One day soon I'll forgive you but, before then, I've got a lot of thinking to do.'

'Wha…?' Pia and Lucie's mouths and eyes were full of confusion.

'I was once asked whether I knew how much a Morgan Three-wheeler cost,' she said to Pia before walking away. 'Now I know. It's a lot. An awful lot.'

chapter thirteen

'How long has she been up there?'

'Two weeks.'

Dan and Patrizia were standing at the St Johns' back door, looking out to the cubby house at the bottom of the backyard. Dan had heeded his and Cara's folks' advice to stay away as long as possible, but it had been the most wretched time of his life. He had been worried sick and pining for her so hard it hurt to breathe. Now he was here, and wouldn't leave until he knew exactly where he stood, and she knew that he hadn't meant to hurt her.

He truly had done it all so that they could be together, but his intent had been lost in the mechanics of the deceit. Cara thought it was a joke but it had, in actual fact, been total desperation, the last resort. One great, final acting job with the best pay he'd ever have.

'What has she been doing?'

'Well, when she came home she sat James and I down and we had a big talk. A lot of hugging, a lot of crying. You know.' Dan nodded and she continued. 'Then she started grabbing stuff and taking it out to the cubby house. The folding stretcher, her old desk, the manual typewriter, all of James's books…and she's been there since. She comes out for meals, but doesn't say much. From what I gather, she's been doing a lot of reading, a lot of writing, but mostly, a lot of thinking.'

'Has she mentioned me?'

'No.'

Dan stood, hands on hips, chewing on his lower lip. He had bided his time long enough. It was time to see her and put an end to the agony. He set out across the velvety lawn.

'Dan! Wait!' Patrizia called.

'It's OK, Pat, I promise I won't upset her.'

It was just like old times as he grasped the ladder and began the climb up the oak tree, glancing upwards at the deceivingly rickety-looking wooden structure set among the thick branches. He was about to pound impatiently on the door with the palm of his hand, when he remembered the code. He clenched his fist and softly knocked out the pattern that told her it was friend, not foe. Tap-tap-tap, tap-tap, tap-tap-tap, tap, tap-tap.

The door opened and there was Cara, lovely and desirable and all he ever wanted – even with the baggy clothes, dark circles under her eyes, and a smear of chocolate at one corner of her mouth.

'Hi, Dan.'

'Hi,' he said softly, 'can I come in?'

'It depends. Do you know the password?'

'I love you.'

'That's not it.'

'I love you anyway.'

She sighed and gave him a small smile. 'All right, I suppose that'll do.'

She moved away from the door and he entered the cubby, noting that the last time he'd been here, he hadn't needed to duck. He accepted her invitation to sit and did so, rather uncomfortably, on the edge of the stretcher.

'We need to talk,' he said. Actually, although he knew they needed to talk, he didn't really want to. All he wanted was to kiss, and touch, and hold, and never ever let go.

'Yeah. So – how are you?' she asked after a brief pause.

'Fine. And you?'

'Fine. How was the speech at Toongalla High?'

Ah, the speech. He cleared his throat. 'Well, it depends on your point of view. I thought the riot I caused was a great reception to it. Ray Coulter, however, wasn't so impressed.'

Cara's smile was incredulous. 'A riot? What happened?'

'Basically? I told them what the teachers told me when I told them my dreams. Then I told them what they'd told you when you'd told them *your* dreams. Then I told them what they'd done to your Dad at the Career Fair, and then…I told them that if they were told anything similar, they should tell the offending teacher to get stuffed.'

'Dan! You didn't!' Cara laughed in both shock and delight.

Eventually the laughter died away and there was a silent pause as Cara looked at the floor. Dan took advantage of the break in her gaze to look at her, the mad blend of hope and fear, restraint and longing, pain and love, coursing through him seizing his words. There was so much he wanted to say…but just one thing he *had* to say.

'Cara, I'm so sorry.'

Cara smiled, then sighed. 'Thank you. I supposed I've already forgiven you, but I still needed to hear it – I don't know why.'

'Your pound of flesh?'

'Maybe. Is it too much to ask? I could have been in real trouble on the island with that knock on the head.'

'Well, actually, Dad gave you a really good check up when you fell. A bit of concussion, that's all you had. Besides, I was there to keep an eye on you, and the ambulance helicopter was just fifteen minutes away.' Dan looked down. He was muffing this, he knew it. He wanted to apologise, and already it seemed like he was making excuses. But he just wanted Cara to understand that he'd never, ever, put her in any real danger.

'Yeah. Well,' Cara paused, then looked up, sad-eyed. 'I wish Pia and Lucie had rung or come so we could talk about all this. I trusted them, and...I just feel that an apology needs to be said so we can go on.'

'Pia and Lucie? Why?' Dan didn't understand. Had they done or said something he hadn't heard about?

'For helping you out, of course. Getting me to go out on that drive in the first place.'

Dan laughed. 'Oh, that! They had nothing to do with it.'

'What?'

'Norman Winston and his little Morgan Three-wheeler would have found you no matter where you were driving. He was Plan B, you see, should the worst happen and you refused to stick around for the week. You did, and so he did.'

'Oh, no.' Cara put her hand on her forehead and closed her eyes. 'My best friends, and I accused them of betrayal.'

Dan smiled and reached into his pocket, retrieving the gift that Pia and Lucie had sent with him. 'I wouldn't worry about it if I were you. They rang me when you went away, and we all got together at Lucie's place and I told them everything.'

'Do they hate me?'

'You tell me. They sent you this.' Dan passed the parcel across to Cara and watched the smile dawn on her face as she unwrapped the tissue paper to reveal a fire-engine red suspender belt. 'So...' he ventured as he watched her wrap it up again, 'is there any chance of me seeing you in it?'

'No.'

He swore and stood up, but only succeeded in bashing

his head against the ceiling, so he swore again, and sat down again. Swiftly, Cara crossed the distance between them and knelt down in front of him, eyes sparkling with tears. She took his face in her hands and gazed into his eyes, reading them for understanding.

'Dan, settle down. It's OK. I know you love me, and I know I love you.'

Hope kindled in his heart, brightening his face. 'You do?'

'Yes.' She smiled.

'But?'

'But…I'm not ready. Look at me! At the moment, I'm not good for anyone, not you, not me. I need to find out who I am again, Dan. Can you understand that? Can you understand that before I give myself to you, I need to make a gift of myself – to me?' She ran a hand through her curls in exasperation. 'I know that for someone who makes a living out of words I'm not making much sense, but please trust me. For us to start something now would be settling for less. Are you willing to hang in there and maybe wait for something better? I can't tell you what I'll have to offer when this mess in my head is sorted out, or whether things will be any easier for us, but will you at least just be patient a little while longer?'

He sighed. She was promising him nothing, and she was promising him everything. There was nothing for it now but to trust his gut. And, although his gut was now twisted and hurting with the pain of loving her, wanting her, and not having her, it had always told him they were meant to be together.

'OK. Just a little while, mind you. Absolutely not one second longer than the rest of my life.'

Cara pumped the lift button in the Crystal Bay Hotel, silently willing it to hurry up. It had been twelve weeks since Cara had kissed Dan goodbye at the door of the cubby house, fighting the overwhelming urge to ask him to stay. While her mind understood that starting something at that moment would mean exchanging the golden future for the fleeting pleasure of the now, her heart did not. It had all but broken as she watched the only man she had ever loved walk away, slouching under the weight of all the uncertainty she had lumbered him with.

But she had needed the time. Heavens, how she'd needed it!

At first, she had grieved and grieved for the person she had been, mentally kicking herself a thousand times for not grabbing and biting at life with gusto, as Marie did. As she had always wanted to do, but had been afraid to. Then she had realised that she'd been given a second chance, and begun to do the necessary reconstruction work – on the inside.

It had been the hardest twelve weeks of her life – and also the most rewarding. She hadn't gone back to the *Clarion* and, amazingly, had experienced none of the withdrawal symptoms she'd always had when away from her desk longer than twenty four hours. In fact, she didn't care at all. She was laughing, catching up with old school friends, riding around Toongalla on her old bicycle, reading, having hour-long telephone conversations with Pia and Lucie…and writing.

Even though she knew that Hutch didn't give a damn, she had actually tried to get the 'week in the life' article down on paper. But it was useless. It had taken on a life of its own as soon as she put her fingers on the typewriter keys. Dan's madcap plan to win her back became the basis for a fantasy that came to life on the page, words flowing out of her like a magical spring. She could not have made this stuff up if she'd tried. The international sex symbol who loved and wanted her and no other, and the wild measures he employed to ensure she stayed close by and gave love a chance to blossom again, right down to a fake stranding on a not-so-deserted island.

She had kept and kept on writing, until all of a sudden here it was in a manuscript box under her arm – 'Fool's Paradise', a quirky love story that no sane person would ever believe had basis in real life. It had been a long time since she had dreamed of creating worlds of make-believe, and an even longer time since she had actually done it. She could not have imagined the healing that writing this story would bring her, for as the words flowed out of her, they seemed to flow life into her. Ray Coulter be damned. Even if by some infinitesimal, hell-freezing-over chance he was right, and writing was not a 'real' job, it didn't matter. It made her feel mighty real.

Crazy Dan and his crazy schemes. He hadn't changed her, but he had somehow fixed it so that she could become reacquainted with herself and her dreams. Re-acquainted, she found out that she and her dreams still really liked each other. That is, some of her dreams. She had more of them, and didn't know how they could possibly come true. She still wanted Dan, still wanted the family. All that ordinary, run-of-the-mill, bourgeois, narcissistic, perfectly wonderful stuff.

It was time for her and Dan to talk.

She raised her hand and knocked softly on the door. Friend or foe? Tap-tap-tap, tap-tap, tap-tap-tap, tap, tap-tap.

Dan was so fast flinging the door open and pulling her into his arms that he was almost a blur. But there was nothing insubstantial in his kisses, however, all over her face, her neck, her hair, hot and desperate and hungry and contagiously so, she discovered as she flung her own arms around him and kissed him back, good as she got.

Eventually they both came up for air and simply gazed at each other, foreheads touching.

'Are you here for good?' he asked.

'Yes.'

'You love me?'

'More than ever.'

'Marry me?'

'Yes…'

'But?'

Cara entered the room and sat down, hands clasped in front of her. She looked up at him with pleading eyes. 'Dan, how do we do this? I mean – I'm not sure I can go back to Los Angeles with you and share the life you've been living all these years. And I can't ask you to give it all up for me either.'

Dan crossed his arms and looked down at her, a funny smile on his face. 'Come with me,' he finally said, pulling her up.

'Where are we…?'

'Just come.'

Dan was silent as he bundled her into a taxi, and all the way to the suburb of Stockton. *Old, established Stockton, with its air of genteel decay*, she thought, head on his comfortably solid shoulder, as they drove through dappled streets lined with tall, manicured hedges that hid venerable brick-and-stone mansions.

The taxi stopped outside a huge Italianate mansion. She could easily imagine what it would have looked like in Victorian times, shining like a jewel in the night, receiving elegant ladies and witty gentlemen into its gleaming wood interiors, the lace covering every surface a perfect echo of that on swishing skirts and stiff shirt cuffs. Now, it appeared that someone was busy trying to restore the place to at least some of its former glory. A renovator's van was parked in the driveway, and paint-spattered workmen milled about carrying tools, climbing up and down ladders, and generally banging about.

'What is this place?' Cara asked.

'Remember Miss Hargreaves?' Dan smiled.

'Who?'

'Miss "Diversional Therapy" Hargreaves?'

'Oh, yeah,' she nodded, remembering the one-woman guerrilla, fighting against the evils of the name 'Jolly Trolley'. But Dan had got Anna to sort her out – yet more of his string-pulling. 'What's she got to do with this?'

Dan put a hand around Cara's waist and led her up the crunchy gravel driveway. 'Well, Anna always said everyone has his or her price. In Miss Hargreaves' case it was this house. You're looking at what it cost to have the cart renamed the "Jolly Trolley".'

'You mean you bought this?'

Dan nodded. 'The market's down and she'd had it up for sale for five years. She was desperate to move down to Melbourne to be closer to her niece.'

'Wow! Talk about disposable income.'

'Not really. Actually, it suited my purposes.'

'Purposes? You have more purposes?'

Dan pointed at the porch wall, and she looked. It was a brass plaque. A brass plaque with Dan's full name on it.

Except that his name had a 'Dr' in front of it.

And lot of letters underneath it.

She squinted at the plaque, as if trying to decipher hieroglyphics. Could it be…?

'You're a doctor?' Cara finally gasped.

'Well, I got my degree just before I left for the US.'

'But…' Cara shook her head, trying to comprehend. This wasn't her Dan, was it? And yet – it obviously was. 'Why didn't I know this?'

'As you can imagine, both our mums were dying to tell you I'd followed in Dad's footsteps.' He rolled his eyes and smiled. 'But I told them not to, for the same reason I left this revelation until now. All I've ever wanted was for you to love me for what I was – even if what I am is a pain in the bum.' He stroked the line of her jaw with his thumb. 'Believe me, since I made it in Hollywood, I've had several lifetimes' share of people wanting to get close to me for what I do.'

'But…I did the research on you. I found nothing about you studying medicine!'

Dan threw his head back and laughed. 'Come on, Cara. You know the score. The publicity machine only lets out what it wants to let out and, in my case, the education was irrelevant. According to my agent, there's nothing the US public hates more than a dilettante. They love the illusion that an actor is born into the profession. So it wasn't worth mentioning, unless I was an Ivy-leaguer.'

Cara put her hands on her hips, shaking her head incredulously.

'So, what are you telling me? You're going to go from being "Mikhail McHale, Double Agent" to being Dr Kildare in one fell swoop?'

'I wish! Actually, I have a lot of work ahead of me. Right now, I just have the very basics, and couldn't practice medicine if I wanted to. But that's going to change. I'm home for good and I'm going back to school, Cara. I'm going to be a paediatrician. A good one. One that makes a real difference.'

Cara's mouth dropped open in unison with her arms, palms upwards. She tried to find words, or even coherent thoughts, but it took some doing.

'But…how…?' She could just see the headlines now! 'You can't just go back to school! At this stage in your career, the media would move in on your university and make things impossible for you!'

'Impossible? You're saying "impossible" to a man who arranged a car crash to get his favourite journalist to interview him, gave the kiss of death to her other relationship, and arranged for her to be stuck on an island with him?'

She looked up at him from lowered lashes and smiled.

'Well, you only did those things because you're hard-headed...'

'Yes...'

'Stubborn...'

'Yes...'

'Persistent...'

'Yes...'

'Obsessive...'

'Yes to all of the above, gorgeous. You know what all those things are about? Passion. Passion is something you feel when you know that something is totally, undeniably right. That is why I am passionate about you. My passion never died all these years because all my life I have known that you and I, we are *right*. And my work with children is also right. I will do whatever it takes to get there, Cara, even if it means bodily fighting off your colleagues in between lectures.'

'But...why now? Why this sudden interest in becoming a paediatrician?'

'Not so sudden,' Dan shook his head. 'Even though I always wanted to make people laugh, I wanted to be a doctor too. I just didn't know how I was going to combine the two – until several months ago. Filming on "Mikhail McHale" had just wrapped up, and even though it was my last contracted picture with the studio, I was fed up to the back teeth with all of it, totally burned out. Everyone wanted a piece of me, and not even total control over the film gave me satisfaction. And, on top of everything, I knew that every second I spent living that life took me further away from you. There had to be more, but I didn't know what it was or how to go about getting it.' He grinned. 'Then, one day, it all clicked. I was in a restaurant into my third beer, when this guy pulled up a chair and said he knew all about my "deep dark secret", and that it was time he used it to make himself some money.'

'Blackmail?' Cara gasped.

'Yeah, that's what I thought too,' Dan chuckled, 'until he introduced himself. It was Alistair Hughes, and right then and there he recruited me into HTICH.' He sighed and looked down at her tenderly. 'Together with you, it's my future.'

'Oh! You…' Cara paused, speechless, then play-slapped his arm. Dan laughed, trying to defend himself. 'Why didn't you tell me?'

'Ow! Would it have made a difference if I had?'

'Yes…no. Yes. No, I'm lying. It wouldn't have.' She knew she hadn't been ready for Dan – in any guise. Her heart had been so wrapped up in hurt and artifice that she would have fought her feelings even if the Archangel Gabriel had revealed the truth to her with a blast from his trumpet. She had been living a life that didn't allow room for either Dan or her real self. It had needed shaking up. Demolishing, even. Dan – her very own demolition man.

'Good,' Dan smiled. 'I didn't want it to.'

Cara looked down. Wings of hope had begun to flutter in her heart, but still she bit her lip. Her own dreams were multi-faceted and surely, Dan's would be too.

'But – what about your comedy?' she finally said, earnestly. She knew what it was like to give up part of yourself for someone else. She couldn't ask Dan to give up anything for her, not if she wanted a real future with him. 'You love it!'

'My comedy is what will make me a good doctor, as it happens. I'm relying on it! But I won't ever completely leave comedy as an art form. I'll still be writing and maybe producing every few years or so. Foster the home-grown talent, and all that. The acting's out of my system, Cara. Right now I'm just interested in one role. "Happily married to the love of my life with a gaggle of children and a job that makes a difference".' He tilted his head, and smiled down at her. 'So, what do you reckon?'

Cara flung her arms around Dan's neck and jumped, wrapping her legs around his waist.

'You're on!'

epilogue

Two years later – give or take a few weeks

'No, I will *not* do it.'

'Oh, come on, Cara,' Marie entreated, trying to stretch as far as she could in her chair. 'I only want to feel your tummy.'

Cara groaned. The small of her back was killing her. 'You'll just have to wait until Dalton's finished, Marie. Until then, I'm not moving one millimetre from this chair.'

'Oh…!' Marie made a noise of disappointment.

'Do what she says!' Dalton chided, brandishing a curling wand like the Statue of Liberty. 'You asked for the curls, remember? Now keep still!'

'Could you have the baby soon?' Marie asked Cara with morbid fascination, as Dalton continued winding and pressing her hair into a springy mass.

'I hope so. I'm into my eleventh month and I've had enough already.'

Dan bent down and kissed her nose. 'You're not exaggerating just a little teeny-weenie bit, are you?'

'You might well be the doctor,' Cara said, shifting to ease the pain, 'but I'm carrying this kid and I say I've been carrying it for at least eleven months.'

'Fine, fine.' He rolled his eyes and grinned. 'Who am I to argue?'

'Cara?' Marie asked. 'Who'll be taking over the workshops at the hospital when you have your baby?'

Cara managed a smile despite the decidedly stronger pain. 'How about you?'

Marie placed a hand on her chest and smiled with delight. 'Me?'

'Well, why not? You're a good writer and living proof of the good a journal can do. And the kids would love to get the low-down from one of their own.'

'All right, I will!'

'I'm glad you like the idea...' Cara suddenly gasped as she found herself in the grip of a fierce contraction.

'Dan...' she managed to whisper at last. '

'Cara...? Sweetheart? Are you OK?'

Cara managed a gritted-teeth smile through the next pain, in a vain effort to reassure Dan, whose worried face was looking most un-doctorlike.

'Yes, darling, I...I'm fine. But...but you'd better get the bags. Call the parents, both sets. I'll be waiting right here. Pia! Lucie!' she added as Dan launched forth to fulfil his pre-fatherly duties, Dalton and Marie hot on his heels.

Pia and Lucie appeared bearing a tray loaded with what would have been a lovely afternoon tea.

'Forget it, girls. Something's come up. Or should I say coming down...?'

Pia and Lucie looked at Cara, then at each other. Both screamed simultaneously.

'Oh-my-gosh! Oh-my-gosh! Get the essential oils! Get the video camera!' Pia yelled, shaking her hands and moving from side-to-side.

Dan appeared, and both Pia and Lucie pushed him out of the door. 'Get the car started. We'll meet you out there.'

'But...but you can't come with us. It'll already be crowded with our folks in there...' Dan protested.

'So?' Lucie was uncharacteristically assertive, daring Dan to contradict her.

'Well, er...'

With an effort, Cara hauled herself to her feet, and placed a hand on Dan's cheek. 'Darling, accept it. Everyone's been waiting for this for a long time, and if you think that it's going to involve just you and me, you really are living in a fool's paradise!'

Dan sighed, then smiled at the family and friends gathered around in nervous happiness. 'OK everyone, pile into the car. Let's get this show on the road.'

He picked Cara up and kissed her once more. 'I'm no fool, and although this paradise is rather more populated than the last one, I know that it's *just* what the doctor ordered!'

Forthcoming titles from HEARTLINE:

OPPOSITES ATTRACT by Kay Gregory
Although *he* doesn't realise it, Venetia Quinn has been in love with her boss, Caleb, ever since he hired her. To Caleb, she's just one of the boys...but a passion filled night has consequences which neither of them could have anticipated...

DECEPTION by June Ann Monks
As a result of his childhood, Ben has always taken a serious approach to life, so 'Kathy Lam's' arrival – she faints in his arms – makes him realise what he's been missing. 'Kathy' has loved Ben all of her life, but what will happen when he discovers that she's been deceiving him?

TROUBLE AT THE TOP by Louise Armstrong
Highly ambitions and fast-moving Nikki has been appointed to close down a once successful business. The one man who stands in her way is gorgeous and sexy Alexander Davidson...definitely a force to be reckoned with!

APPLES FOR THE TEACHER by Steffi Gerrard
Ellie is an experienced teacher of adults, but finds it incredibly difficult to cope with Chris Martin – the most extraordinary handsome and sexy man she's ever met. In fact, it isn't long before Ellie is beginning to wonder if Chris Martin is all that he seems.

Why not start a new romance today with Heartline Books. We will send you an exciting Heartline romance ABSOLUTELY FREE. You can then discover the benefits of our home delivery service: Heartline Books Direct.

Each month, before they reach the shops, you will receive four brand new titles, delivered directly to your door.

All you need to do, is to fill in your details opposite – and return them to us at the Freepost address.

Please send me my free book:

Name (IN BLOCK CAPITALS)

_____

Address (IN BLOCK CAPITALS)

_____

_____

_____

_____ Postcode _____

Address:
HEARTLINE BOOKS
FREEPOST LON 16243,
Swindon SN2 8LA

We may use this information to send you offers from ourselves or
selected companies, which may be of interest to you.

If you do not wish to receive further offers
from Heartline Books, please tick this box ☐

If you do not wish to receive further offers
from other companies, please tick this box ☐

Once you receive your free book, unless we hear from you otherwise,
within fourteen days, we will be sending you four exciting new romantic
novels at a price of £3.99 each, plus £1 p&p. Thereafter, each time you
buy our books, we will send you a further pack of four titles.

You can cancel at any time! You have no obligation to ever buy a
single book.

Heartline Books –
romance at its best!

What do you think of this month's selection?

As we are determined to continue to offer you books which are up to the high standard we know you expect from Heartline, we need you to tell us about *your* reading likes and dislikes. So can we please ask you to spare a few moments to fill in the questionnaire on the following pages and send it back to us? And don't be shy – if you wish to send in a form for each title you have read this month, we'll be delighted to hear from you!

Questionnaire

Please tick the boxes to indicate your answers:

1   Did you enjoy reading this Heartline book?

    Title of book: _____

    A lot   ☐
    A little   ☐
    Not at all ☐

2   What did you particularly like about this book?

    Believable characters   ☐
    Easy to read   ☐
    Enjoyable locations   ☐
    Interesting story   ☐
    Good value for money   ☐
    Favourite author   ☐
    Modern setting   ☐

3   If you didn't like this book, can you please tell us
    why?

    _____

    _____

4 Would you buy more Heartline Books each month if they were available?

Yes ☐

No – four is enough ☐

5 What other kinds of books do you enjoy reading?

Historical fiction ☐

Puzzle books ☐

Crime/Detective fiction ☐

Non-fiction ☐

Cookery books ☐

Other _____

_____

6 Which magazines and/or newspapers do you read regularly?

a) _____

b) _____

c) _____

d) _____

And now a bit about you:

Name _____

Address _____

_____

_____ Postcode _____

Thank you so much for completing this questionnaire.
Now just tear it out and send it in an envelope to:

HEARTLINE BOOKS
PO Box 400
Swindon SN2 6EJ

(and if you don't want to spoil this book, please feel free
to write to us at the above address with your comments
and opinions.)

Code: FP

Have you missed any of the following books:

The Windrush Affairs *by Maxine Barry*
Soul Whispers *by Julia Wild*
Beguiled *by Kay Gregory*
Red Hot Lover *by Lucy Merritt*
Stay Very Close *by Angela Drake*
Jack of Hearts *by Emma Carter*
Destiny's Echo *by Julie Garrett*
The Truth Game *by Margaret Callaghan*
His Brother's Keeper *by Kathryn Bellamy*
Never Say Goodbye *by Clare Tyler*
Fire Storm *by Patricia Wilson*
Altered Images *by Maxine Barry*
Second Time Around *by June Ann Monks*
Running for Cover *by Harriet Wilson*
Yesterday's Man *by Natalie Fox*
Moth to the Flame *by Maxine Barry*
Dark Obsession *by Lisa Andrews*
Once Bitten…Twice Shy *by Sue Dukes*
Shadows of the Past *by Elizabeth Forsyth*
Perfect Partners *by Emma Carter*
Melting the Iceman *by Maxine Barry*
Marrying A Stranger *by Sophie Jaye*
Secrets *by Julia Wild*
Special Delivery *by June Ann Monks*
Bittersweet Memories *by Carole Somerville*
Hidden Dreams *by Jean Drew*
The Peacock House *by Clare Tyler*
Crescendo *by Patricia Wilson*
The Wrong Bride *by Susanna Carr*
Forbidden *by Megan Paul*
Playing with Fire *by Kathryn Bellamy*
Collision Course *by Joyce Halliday*
Illusions *by Julia Wild*
It Had To Be You *by Lucy Merritt*
Summer Magic *by Ann Bruce*
Imposters In Paradise *by Maxine Barry*

Complete your collection by ringing the Heartline Hotline on 0845 6000504, visiting our website www.heartlinebooks.com or writing to us at Heartline Books, PO Box 400, Swindon SN2 6EJ